JUNE FOSTER

All Things New

Woodlyn, Book 3

By June Foster

Copyright © 2018 by June Foster

Forget Me Not Romances, a division of Winged Publications.

All rights reserved as permitted under the U.S. Copyright Act of 1976. No part of the publication may be reproduced, distributed or transmitted in any form or by any means, or stored in a database or retrieval system, without prior permission of the publisher.
This book is a work of fiction. Names, characters, places, and incidents are the product of the author's imagination and are used fictitiously. Any resemblance to actual events, locales, or persons, living or dead, is coincidental.

ISBN-13: 979-8-8691-0592-9
:

Chapter One

"Yes, Mom, I miss you, too." Jillian Coleman hoisted her purse on her shoulder and grasped the little sack with the two baby gifts.

"When can you get back to New York for a visit?"

Mom's tender voice sent a ripple of longing through Jillian—to see her parents. But not only that, to feel a part of a family again.

Family. She longed for one of her own—a husband and kids. With a gulp, she acknowledged the question demanding her attention. Would God allow it after what she did? "I can't afford to take time off from the hospital right now. I've got at least six patients who'll deliver in the next couple of months, and they're counting on me." Jillian took a few steps toward the front door. "Maybe I can come home Christmas."

"Jillian, you know how much your father and I love you. We pray for you every day."

"I need your prayers. I love you both, too." Jillian repositioned the cell phone on her ear. "Mom, I need to go in a minute. I'm off to a double baby shower for two of my expectant mothers."

"Another one? Sweetie, you're the most caring obstetrician in the city of Woodlyn. No wonder your patients always invite you."

"That's nice of you to say."

"Honey, do you ever wish..."

Wish for a baby of her own? She didn't have to read Mom's mind to know what she planned to say. "More than I want to admit." In the entry, Jillian slumped against the wall. "I dream of holding my little boy or girl, wrapped in a pink or blue blanket, asleep in my arms. But, Mom, don't count on being a grandmother anytime soon, if ever. I don't think it's going to happen."

~

Riley Mathis never thought he'd park in front of a church, much less attend a service inside. The red brick building with the towering steeple perched on top seemed like home now. *Almost.* The old Chevy sputtered when he turned off the engine.

The extra cars on a Saturday in the parking lot puzzled him. Maybe he had the wrong day. Was the pastor having a meeting? He should pull on around and disappear out the opposite entrance.

No. He had to mow the grass. Couldn't procrastinate another week. Anyway, the event didn't involve him, though he wouldn't mind getting acquainted with some folks besides Tim Garrett. Except they probably wouldn't want to know him. Not when they found out about his past—where he'd spent the last ten years. He'd do his work and leave.

The grass in front of the building didn't appear overgrown, but it wouldn't hurt to mow before the lawn got too high. He wanted to serve the Lord and take care of God's property. Do the best job he could though he hadn't always thought that way. Now he lived to please God more than man. At least that expressed his heart's desire. Whether he could live up to the standards... well, he had to try. The yard in back bordering the woodland would definitely need attention.

Tim had the keys to the maintenance shed in his office. Riley would get them and head out back for the lawnmower. The covered entrance through the double glass doors led down the hall in that direction.

The laughter and chatter of feminine voices wafted from the fellowship hall when he walked through the front door. He poked his head into the large room.

Tammy, Evergreen's efficient secretary, stood with one hand on her hip and pointed to the long tables in the back of the room. Another lady he'd seen at the services faced her and gestured toward the front wall nearest the door.

"Hey, Riley."

He circled around to the voice behind him. Tim Garrett, just the guy he needed to see. "Hey, buddy. I came by for the keys. I'm going to tackle that jungle out back this afternoon."

"Thanks. Since you didn't show up last week, the grass is pretty high."

"Yeah, uh..." Riley had no excuse except procrastination. *Wait until tomorrow or the next day. Who cared?* He gave himself a mental shake. That was the old Riley thinking. "Sorry, Tim."

"You're here now." Tim turned his head to the voices in the fellowship hall. "I think there's going to be an event here this afternoon." He scratched the back of his neck and offered a sheepish grin. "A double baby shower and you'll never guess who one of the expectant mothers is."

Riley laughed. "Hmm. Don't tell me. I spotted an invitation on the bulletin board for... *hmmm*. Holly Colton." He enjoyed giving Tim a hard time, he had to admit.

Tim jabbed him in the ribs. "A double shower, man. My wife is having a baby too. You know that."

"Just gotta kid you a little." He shrugged away the discomfort creeping up his shoulders. "Hey, dude. I don't have much experience with women and babies." *Probably never would.* He'd muddled his life so bad he'd never subject someone else to sharing it.

"Your day will come, buddy." Tim smirked and cupped a hand on his mouth. "If you want the truth, I have no idea how to change a diaper, though Jess Colton said he'd give me lessons."

Tammy dragged a chair from one of the tables in the back and set it toward the front of the room. She smiled. "Hey, you guys. We need a couple of sets of muscles here. Could we impose on you two?"

Riley glanced at Tim and lifted an eyebrow. "Sure. Be happy to help out. As long as I'm out of here when Roxanne and Holly start opening all that baby stuff." He shuddered. "I don't do bottles and diapers."

"Don't worry, I just need for you men to move those two tables up front here to the wall and make about half of those chairs into a large circle." She pointed toward the front of the room. "Stack the rest against the far wall next to the kitchen. Oh, yeah. Hang the banner over the gift table. All of that before the guests begin to arrive." The church secretary giggled. "And that's all."

Tim cut his eyes toward Riley. "No problem."

They marched toward the long rows. Tim picked up one end of the rectangular table, and Riley grabbed the other, moving it up front along the wall. They placed the next table beside it. After they put the chairs in a large circle, they taped a banner over the first table with *Congratulations, Holly and Roxanne* in pink letters and pictures of baby rattles and those little shoes infants wear.

Tammy emerged from the kitchen and set a large tray of fruit and a basket of crackers on the food table. "Thanks. You guys are great."

"Any time ladies." Tim picked up an old Sunday bulletin from the floor and tossed it in the garbage receptacle.

A good-looking woman carrying two packages wrapped in white paper with a pink bow on each glided through the door toward them.

Riley didn't want to stare, but the tall lady with shoulder length auburn hair and aquamarine-blue eyes looked familiar. *Hmm, where have I seen her before?* Something about her face…

She strolled toward Tammy, then set the gifts on the first table now covered with a white cloth.

Oh, man, I've got to stop gawking at her. This was ridiculous, but her presence bugged him. She must be someone…from his past. Someone who was more than an acquaintance.

Tim grasped four unneeded folding chairs and hauled them to where the others were stacked. Three more chairs rested against the wall between the food table and the kitchen a few feet from Tammy who chatted with the woman.

If Riley wanted to take those chairs to the back with

the others, he had to walk right by them. Steeling his nerves, he gawked at his tennis shoes as he trudged across the tile. Then he froze in place. A sapphire necklace on the lady's throat glistened with the rays from the ceiling lights.

As if a magnet drew him, Riley inched closer, first staring at her beautiful face, then allowing his gaze to travel down her neck with the blue sapphire surrounded by a row of diamonds hanging from a silver chain. How many other necklaces were like that one? It had to be a one-of-a-kind. *Dear Lord. Surely not.* He swallowed the groan that tried to escape his throat. She couldn't be the same person from that night so long ago, the girl who wore an identical necklace. Could she? The innocent girl he'd shown no regard for -- who'd only represented another conquest.

He'd never forget. How could he? The necklace had preyed upon his dreams for years. Riley couldn't calm his quivering hands.

Again he peered at the jewelry gracing her long white throat. When he looked up, to his dismay, the shapely woman glared at him.

Someone grasped his arm. "Hey, Riley. You're slacking off." Tim tugged his elbow.

Squeezing his eyes shut didn't help sweep away the cobwebs from his past. He carried the remaining three chairs and stacked them with the others.

Tim's eyebrows, in the shape of a V, gave Riley the clue. He'd messed up. With a wide sweep of his arm, Tim motioned him back where the two ladies still conversed. "Uh, Jillian, may I introduce my friend and fellow church member, Riley Mathis. Riley, Dr. Jillian Coleman."

"It's…uh, nice to meet you Dr. Coleman." Should he shake hands with her? He stuck out his palm. It hovered in the air a moment. He pulled it back when she frowned at him. "I was… noticing your necklace." How stupid did that sound? He'd ogled her for five minutes. Nobody would believe he was looking at the jewelry instead of her chest. In fact…he'd more than likely insulted her.

"How do you do?" She turned to Tammy. "If there's anything I can help with, please let me know."

Tim clutched Riley's arm hard. "May I see you in my office, please?" He clipped his whispered words.

Okay, he didn't have the best social skills. After all, he'd missed the chance to live in society for the last ten years since his confinement in the Puhoma Correctional Institute. He cleared his voice. "Yeah, sure." But he knew what his friend would probably say.

Marching down the long corridor to Tim's office wasn't pleasant, especially in Tim's tight grip.

Riley was a school kid in trouble on his way to the principal's office. "Look man, I'm sorry."

The sign below the frosted glass panel at the top of the door read *Tim Garrett, Pastoral Counselor*. "You're probably going to offer me advice, and I'm sure I need it, but…"

Couldn't talk his way out of this one. Riley followed him into his office.

Tim closed the door and glared at Riley. "You've been out of prison now for almost six months. I'm grateful you gave your life to the Lord. Thank God for Chuck Colson's Prison Fellowship Ministry, but..."

"Okay, I have a feeling the *but* is leading to a lecture."

"Must I remind you," Tim held up his palm, "you're on supervised release, which requires participation in a mental health program. You're fortunate the state allowed you to work with me instead of a secular agency."

"I know. I think the only reason was because my monthly drug tests have been clean." Riley tapped his foot.

Tim straightened his shoulders and narrowed his eyes to slits. "That's right. Now... Jillian Coleman is an attractive woman. I have a suspicion she thought you were trying to look at her in an inappropriate way." He ran a hand through his hair. "But I'm wondering if you weren't looking at that expensive piece of jewelry on her neck. Riley, I hate to say this, but you acted like either a letch or a thief." He grasped his shoulder and squeezed. "You've come too far, man, to fall back into past sins."

As if a splash of icy cold water doused him on a frigid winter day, Riley caught his breath. The disgusting truth invaded his awareness. He dreaded telling Tim, but his friend already knew so much about him. He cleared his throat. "No worries, man. Not now. Not anymore. I've already stolen something from that woman, and I'm not proud of it."

His pulse throbbed with the memories, the shape of her eyes, the curve of her lips, her flawless skin. Jillian Coleman -- the woman from his past.

"Look, friend. I don't know the details of what you've confessed to me, but it sounds like a big deal. My door here at church is always open to you. I think we need to talk about this at our next session." Tim issued him a scrutinizing look.

"Yeah. I know… Later, man." Riley grabbed the set of keys to the shed that Tim offered and staggered out of his office. Jillian. A doctor who'd worked hard while he'd sat in a prison cell. If he hadn't made those mistakes trying to have it all, maybe he'd stand a chance with her now. But he'd blown his life on drugs and sex, and even if they didn't have a one-night stand between them, a maintenance worker would never measure up to a doctor.

~

Jillian crossed one leg over the other and sipped the lime-green sparkling drink with a dab of sherbet floating on top. Relaxing her stiff shoulders seemed impossible, but the image of that guy Tim introduced her to staring at her chest brought her pulse rate up again. How dare the jerk ogle her, and in church? Tim had obviously seen the problem and carted the guy out of the room.

The pregnant Roxanne Garrett, her friend and patient, occupied a good portion of the chair next to her. She balanced a plate of cake on top of her stomach, stuck her fork in the sugary dessert, and took a bite.

"Hey, Roxy, what do you know about Riley Mathis…the one who helped Tim with the chairs?"

Roxy shifted on the folding chair, grasping her plate with one hand. "Oh, Riley? He's a nice guy. Tim and I've known him for a while. I think he's been going to Evergreen since last winter. He mows the grass for the church on weekends. Why do you ask?"

"Oh, I don't know." Couldn't bother Roxy with her negative thoughts and suspicions. But something played at the edge of her mind. Something about the way his light brown hair fell on his forehead and those electric blue eyes. What was it? Had she seen him somewhere? Jillian shook her head and brought her thoughts back to Roxy. "It's nothing."

"Roxanne and Holly. Please move up into these two chairs in front. You're our special guests." Tammy put her hand on the back of two folding chairs next to the gift table. "A lot of exciting packages are waiting for you ladies to open."

Roxy patted Jillian's arm, hoisted herself up, and set her plate on the food table. "Talk to you later, my friend."

Diapers, pink nightshirts, baby toys, blankets, and tiny girls' dresses emerged from the boxes and bags. With each new gift, a round of *aw's* and *oo's* sounded through the room.

Infants. How she longed to be more than the doctor who delivered them. If only... She forced the thought away and ran a finger under her eye to wipe away the moisture. Why did she torture herself?

Tammy and Roxanne's mother, Mrs. Ratner, wheeled two baby strollers into the room. A smile sat on Tammy's lips. "Surprise, ladies. We have one more gift for you. Some of us went in together to get you these strollers -- the kind you can use if you want to go jogging with your babies."

Holly and Roxanne gave squeals of delight.

Jillian's churning emotions quieted a bit. Holly had found contentment in her life as a wife and mother. Roxy, barely more than a newlywed, treasured her new role as a soon-to-be-mom. Sharing their joy every time they came in for checkups was easy. But was it enough?

Holly ran her hands along the canvas seat of the grey and black stroller. Both her patients glowed.

Jess, Holly's husband, stepped through the door. "Am I welcome yet?"

Tammy glanced up. "Hey. One of our fathers-to-be. Well, in Jess' case, a father for the second time."

Roxy beamed as Tim strolled into the fellowship hall. "Oh, honey. Look at all the gifts our little girl received." An array of boxes and sacks surrounded her on the table and floor.

Tammy handed Tim a large shopping bag. "For all that loot."

He grinned and stuffed packages of diapers, a baby book, and little pink and yellow night shirts into the sack. Then he looked at Roxanne with adoring eyes.

All Jett did was gawk at her in his possessive way. What would it be like to have her boyfriend gaze at her like Tim did Roxanne? Jillian sighed at the tenderness in Tim's expression.

"Hey, Dr. Coleman." Holly waddled toward Jillian with a smile. "Thank you so much for coming. Timmy's little sister is going to love the baby blankets and the cute booties."

How could Jillian have considered not coming? "My pleasure."

A sprinkling of freckles dotted Holly's nose. "Are you dating that handsome doctor I've seen you talking to between appointments at your office?"

An image of the towering Dr. Jett Camp, with his blond hair slicked back from his forehead, slipped into her mind again. "Yeah. I have to admit I think he's interested in me, with all the flowers and candy he's been sending."

Jillian gave herself a mental pinch. Jett might be interested in her, but how did she feel about him with his clinical demeanor and strongly held opinions about how she should live her life? Though his career seemed to come first, when the handsome guy gave her attention, he could make her pulse pound.

Running her hand over her swollen stomach, Holly squeezed Jillian's hand. "Well, guess I better go help Jess pack up the rest of the presents. I'll see you at my next appointment."

"All right, sweetie." At least she could appreciate the joy of new birth vicariously by bringing babies safely into families like the Coltons and the Garretts. But what about the other young women and girls who'd made unwise choices and found themselves pregnant under the wrong circumstances -- the girls contemplating abortion?

If only she could accomplish her dream of someday operating a free clinic for teenage girls, she could provide the opportunity for many to give birth.

God's message from the book of Jeremiah burned in her mind. "Before I formed you in the womb I knew you, before you were born I set you apart." But *The Jeremiah House* would have to wait for now.

Jillian rose to refill her punch cup but a sip of the liquid didn't take her mind off the cascade of emotions filling her heart. She'd doctor for free if that would prevent one girl from making that deceitful, devastating mistake.

Chapter Two

The morning sun beamed bright, sending shafts of light bouncing off the thick foliage growing in the park. Riley huffed, slowed down, and grabbed his knees to catch his breath. After another puff, he set his legs in motion again. The dirt path, hardened and packed by hundreds of joggers and walkers, curved around a tall Douglas fir into a clearing.

He pulled in a breath of the evergreen-perfumed air. Late May in Washington was glorious, and the freedom to jog through the park meant more than ever now. Prison had denied him that experience for so many years.

The sparkling waters of the Chako Chee Creek flowed over an outcropping of boulders onto flat rocks and into a shallow pool. Though Cascade Waterfall Park lay in the center of downtown Woodlyn, the area had the feel of a wilderness.

Heat radiated on his neck with every thought of yesterday's encounter with Jillian. Like a brainless idiot, he'd given her the impression he ogled her body, when in reality he'd been captivated by her necklace. Even Tim had interpreted the situation the same. He deserved the counselor's rebuke, but he'd never lower himself to steal her necklace, though he'd done something much worse to her. He prayed she'd never remember that night—or him.

A bolt of electricity had traveled down his spine when Jillian's identity hit him. He hadn't respected her years ago, but today he recognized her as an ambitious woman who'd studied to become a physician, a valuable human being. Now, he saw her through the filter of his new beliefs formed by trust in God. *What a difference.* He wiped the sweat off his forehead and rounded another corner.

The waters of the Chako Chee danced in the sunlight, bubbling over small rocks and patches of river moss. A blue jay with its top feathers waving in the breeze flitted through the air and landed near the slender fronds of a fern.

Up ahead, the path bent into a stand of Douglas fir.

About a hundred yards beyond, a woman jogged toward him.

His knees wobbled. *Jillian.* He caught his breath. How could she be here now, for Pete's sake? What were the chances of Jillian jogging in the park at the same time as him in the large community of Woodlyn? *Hmm. It is Sunday and a gorgeous afternoon.* Stood to reason the doctor would enjoy getting away from work once in a while.

With her head down, she stared at the path, her focus probably on the trail.

Good. She hadn't seen him. Riley made a one-eighty. He had no desire to meet up with her. Increasing his pace from a jog to a run, he passed the falls again and caught a glimpse of the commons with the park benches and pole lights interspersed among elm and fir trees. Maybe he should head back to his car.

The sound of whimpering caught his attention. He slowed to a fast walk. A girl about eighteen sat under an elm, her knees to her chest. A cell phone rested in one hand, and she wiped her eyes with the other.

The sight of the teen batting at her cheeks and looking toward the park entrance, as if waiting for somebody to show up, stirred his emotions. Maybe she needed someone to listen to her, to share her problems—so like himself as a youth.

If he'd only had God in his life, he wouldn't have hooked up with those drug dealers trying to make quick money. Even Mom hadn't found the Lord yet, not until after he went to prison. He gave himself a mental boot in the seat of his pants. He couldn't blame anyone else for his stupid mistakes.

Riley peered at the girl. Had she used recently? Her motionless stare could indicate a fuzzy, drug induced state of mind, like those teens he'd sold to. *Lord, you know my desire to minister to teens, the longing you put in my heart.*

With his hands shoved into the pockets of his jogging shorts, he strolled along the path closer to the girl. But if he approached her, she might get the wrong idea.

Jillian. Though meeting up with her again sent a stab of anxiety to his stomach, if she went with him, he could go up to the teen without feeling awkward. Riley turned back the way he came.

In a slow jog, Jillian drew nearer, about fifty yards down the path.

What would she think if he asked her to go along with him? Though she might not be willing after the fiasco at the shower, he could try. The teen's welfare was more important than his embarrassment in facing Jillian again. He kicked a rock out of the path, and picked up his pace.

Her ponytail swayed from side to side each time her tennis shoe hit the path. She panted, then lifted her chin. Her eyes snagged him and widened, a smile absent from her lips. With a glance behind her, she slowed the pace of her jog. Maybe she was considering turning around to avoid him.

"Dr. Coleman, Jillian, hold up." He jogged nearer. "I…I need to apologize about yesterday." He blurted the words between short gasps of breath caused more by his nerves than his jogging, and clutched his throat. "I have no excuse other than your necklace… *someone* I knew long ago had one like it."

She scrunched her brow, fingered the same piece of jewelry around her neck, and tucked it inside her tee shirt.

"Hey, I'm not really Jack the Ripper. I'm sorry I gave you the wrong impression." He swiped a hand through his hair. His conscience poked him because his words were deceptive. That *someone* was Jillian, but no way could he tell her.

She jogged to a stop in front of him. "Okay. That's fine." She pulled in a breath. "We'll chalk it up to a misunderstanding. Besides, Roxanne Garrett assured me you were a friendly guy." Her face softened. "So you're making Evergreen Fellowship your home church? I don't think I've seen you there."

"Uh, yeah. I'm gradually feeling like I belong." He didn't remember seeing her either and wouldn't tell the doctor he'd been attending only since he got out of prison. "Look, Jillian. I need to ask you a favor. I saw a girl farther up the path sitting under a tree crying, near the commons. I want to help her if I can. You know, kind of like a ministry thing. Do you suppose you could go with me to talk to her?" Heat filled his face. Ten years ago his motives to talk to her were less than honorable. "I think a woman would make her feel more relaxed. She might open up to you."

As if the thick foliage bordering the path had captured her attention, Jillian looked toward it. Maybe she intended to ignore him. Finally, she turned her face toward him. "Sure. I'd like to."

Riley breathed out a sigh. At least Jillian didn't see him as a philanderer any longer. "Thanks, she's down the path."

They kept a brisk pace around the bend to the commons. "Over there. See her?" He gave his head a sideways nod toward the girl still sitting under the tree. This time she'd hidden her face on her knees.

The teen's presence jangled Riley's nerves. What could he say to her? Another ten yards and they stopped in front of the tree. Riley bent down. A sniffing sound met his ears. "Excuse me."

The girl jerked her head up.

"My friend and I were jogging. We…uh, we both go to the same church. We saw you crying. Is there anything we can help with?"

The teen rubbed her tearstained face with the back of her hand and looked from Riley to Jillian. She shrugged and studied the cell phone still in one hand.

"Believe it or not, we were both teens, too. Whatever you're going through, we understand. We had our share of struggles as well." He couldn't speak for

Jillian although he imagined she had some tough times growing up. Every kid did.

Jillian knelt in front of the girl. "We really care about you and want to help you." She gave Riley a desperate glance.

"That guy said he could understand what I'm going through. There's no way he could." The teen lifted her face to Jillian. "Nothing could save me now, not even God, unless..." She buried her face in her hands and her shoulders shook.

"Honey, there is nothing impossible with God." Jillian placed a hand on her arm. "He can do all things. He understands your situation."

Riley's chest swelled as he watched Jillian speaking to the teen, with compassion, like she really cared about the girl. As he did. Could the Lord have called her to a ministry as well?

"He can't take this baby out of my body. I have to do it." The girl wrenched her hands over her face, and her shoulders shook.

"You're...you're pregnant?" Jillian exhaled a gush of air and drew her hand to her mouth, then the crease lines above her nose released. She patted the girl's arm. "I mean, it's okay, honey. You have more than one option."

"I'm pregnant, all right, but not for long." The teen firmed her mouth. "I'm getting my nerve up to go in for the abortion."

Jillian's jaw gaped. "Oh...No, please don't do that. Please. Listen to me."

Of all people, a Christian obstetrician would understand better than anyone else. The caring look on Jillian's face confirmed his thought.

"Please reconsider." Jillian clasped her hands in front of her mouth. "You can't take the life of your unborn child."

Jillian's plea left Riley's heart aching with sadness for the girl but amazement at Jillian's degree of passion with which she spoke.

The tearful teen folded her arms over her chest. "Look, I've already been to Planned Parenthood. They said it's okay. It's only a blob of tissue. It's not a baby."

"But you said it yourself." Jillian paused and ran a hand across the adolescent's shoulder. "A baby is inside you."

With an intake of breath, she flinched. "I mean, uh…I didn't mean to say that. If my parents ever found out about this, they'd kill me. My mother's into all that society stuff, and my father thinks he's the best lawyer in Woodlyn. I can't be responsible for ruining their lives."

"What about the baby's father?" Jillian patted her hand.

"Yeah, I'd ruin his life, too." A blank expression fell across the girl's face, and she stared straight ahead. "He doesn't care." She spoke with slow, measured tones without expression. "He said he's too busy to be a father. He's going to law school in a couple of years, just like my father. My boyfriend would pay for the abortion, but I've got enough myself."

Jillian's shoulders slumped. "At least tell me your name so I can pray for you. Just your first name."

The girl lowered her head and squeezed her eyes shut. "Jamie."

"Jamie, you wouldn't exist if your mother had aborted you." Jillian took both the teen's hands in hers.

"Don't you want to give your child a chance to live?"

Jamie tugged at her ear. "I…uh…never thought of that."

"I'm a doctor. I deliver babies every day. I can help you." A glow shone in Jillian's eyes. "Be at Woodlyn Physicians for Women on Monday afternoon. It's the large building on Main across the street from Starbucks. My office is on the first floor. Tell the receptionist I asked you to come in."

"I'll think about it." Jamie fingered her cell with two hands. "What's your number?"

The teen entered the digits into her phone as Jillian slowly repeated them.

Jillian folded her hands in front of her. "I can provide medical assistance and put you in touch with an adoption agency if that's what you'd like. Give me yours, too."

"Monday, if I come in." With a wary look, Jamie studied Jillian and squeezed her eyes shut. "Thank you, but I don't think there's another option for me except abortion."

~

Jillian's heart sank as Jamie walked farther away from the park toward the street. But how hard would Jillian have to work to keep her tears from surfacing and rolling down her cheeks? How well she knew the truth. If the young woman went through with her plans, she'd regret it the rest of her life. Knowing God forgives wouldn't erase Jamie's guilt and sorrow.

Nothing would ever take away the memory of the day ten years ago when she wobbled through the front door of the women's clinic, her stomach churning and convulsing. Jillian shuddered. She had lain on a sterile table and allowed the doctor to examine her. The physician had injected a pain killer to minimize her discomfort. A sardonic laugh shot from Jillian's throat.

What about the baby's pain? She hadn't thought of it at the time. In comparison, her own pain seemed minimal now.

Though she tried hard not to think, the scene played relentlessly in her mind. She'd always remember the sound—the *woosh* of the vacuum the doctor used to aspirate the fetus. The thought still sent violent blows to her stomach.

Later she'd listened to the nurse's assurances.

"You're doing the right thing," the woman had said. "This way you can get on with your life."

Jillian had continued on with her life, all right. Nothing to hinder her from going to school, but more than that, her parents never had to know.

Jillian cringed. She got on with her life at the expense of another life? Her baby would be in fifth grade now. What would he or she have offered to the world? A cure for cancer? Or maybe her child would have been her best friend and given her delightful grandchildren.

Anger welled up in her. The nurse had lied. What Jillian did had not been the right thing. The personnel at the clinic betrayed her, feeding her one untruth after another. They never told her about the repercussions.

How many nights of sleep had she lost experiencing the procedure over and over again? Some days she drove to work wondering if her patients would notice the dark circles under her eyes. But in the end, she had no one to blame but herself.

Dear Lord, please allow Jamie to seek help, my help if You want her to. Don't let her make the same mistake I did. Don't allow her to believe the lies that the baby inside her isn't real.

"Hey, you okay?" Riley touched her shoulder. "I'll have to admit, I felt for that girl. In your profession, you're probably reminded all the time that a mother carries a real baby inside and not some kind of tissue."

Jillian peered at Riley, his boyish face gazing down at her, and savored his look of compassion. Her heart warmed. Finally a man who understood her way of thinking.

Though Jett had ignored her when she spoke of her dream—a clinic for girls like Jamie, Riley would probably encourage her.

Encountering Jamie today brought her more determination than ever. The teen not only tugged at her heart, she yanked and jerked it. Jillian had to get her clinic up and going despite what Jett thought.

Riley took a couple of steps toward a park bench. "Sit down for a minute. Maybe we could pray for her."

Pray…with him? Jett had never offered, though she'd never asked him. "That would be great."

A bench sat several yards away from the tree where they'd talked to Jamie only minutes ago. She eased down next to him.

Elbows resting on his knees, he sat motionless for a moment staring at the grass.

Two joggers zipped past, oblivious of the drama that occurred only moments ago, unaware a teen contemplated ending the life of her baby.

Sitting so close to Riley brought Jillian back to their

purpose, to seek the Lord.

Riley closed his eyes. "Lord, you know all things. You see this desperate young woman, and you've heard the lies she's believed. Bring her to her senses and allow the baby within her to live. Use us, Lord. Amen."

His smooth voice brought her peace, though Jamie's situation distressed her. "I agree in prayer, Lord." Yesterday, she'd thought Riley a womanizer or worse. But the guy's heart was in the right place. He loved God and wanted to serve Him, from what she'd observed today. "It's strange I haven't seen you at church before, but I miss sometimes when I'm at the hospital. I don't know too much about you."

The change in Riley's expression perplexed her. A moment before, his face displayed peace, the same calm his prayer brought her. Now he squirmed and cleared his throat.

"Oh, I…uh, take an on-line class and work for my stepfather." He stood. "Look, I need to go. Hope to see you at church." He jogged off in the direction of the parking lot.

Jillian snapped her mouth shut when she realized it hung open. With every step he took, he lifted his shoulder in a peculiar way, as if unsure of his destination. The way he carried himself...like someone she'd known in her past, but she couldn't remember who.

Riley disappeared behind the shrubbery on the other side of the commons. One minute he prayed a beautiful prayer and the next he fled like a criminal. She'd only made a friendly comment. What had happened?

JUNE FOSTER

Chapter Three

Riley shoved through the single door to the corner office building with the sign *Woodlyn Building Maintenance* on the east wall. At least he was on time. The air conditioning cooled his face, still warm from yesterday afternoon's encounter with Jillian. Her simple remark that she didn't know much about him had set him in a panic.

Tim Garrett knew of his past but held it in confidence, though the day would probably come when Riley couldn't keep it a secret any longer. Maybe he should tell others. God had forgiven him. Surely his Christian brothers and sisters would as well.

But the thought of revealing his incarceration to Jillian caused his heart to stop beating. Not only was he ashamed for her to know he'd been put away, but worse, he feared she'd remember their past.

What would she think of him? He'd never get a chance to say he was sorry or get to know her as his Christian sister if she learned the truth.

Gallon size bottles of disinfectant, glass cleaner, and a dozen other janitorial products filled the rows of shelving along the wall in the main office. A floor polisher, Shop-Vac, and mop bucket with a ringer sat against another wall.

Riley turned to his left and perused the work schedule on the bulletin board. Everybody's name but his. He lifted his fist and knocked at Dexter's closed office door.

"Yeah, come in." His stepfather's irritated voice sounded from the other side. *He's not in the best of moods. What can you expect for Monday morning?*

A nervous pang ransacked Riley's stomach before he turned the knob and walked in. Dexter muttered something as he punched the keys of a calculator and glanced back at a paper lying on his desk. He took a quick look at Riley, then returned to stabbing the keys of his machine. "Sit down," he growled.

Moisture gathered on Riley's brow as he slipped into the chair opposite Dexter and laced his fingers, circling his thumbs. If he could fade into the carpet, he would. Why couldn't his boss just give him his weekly assignment so he could get out of here.

Dex switched off the calculator and pushed the paper aside. If his scowl was any indication, he didn't have good news. He ran his hand over his mouth. "My budget's getting tighter. I crunched a few numbers and am going to have to scale back."

Oh, so that's why my name's not on the schedule. He's canning me. Riley's heart pounded hard. His stepfather had done him a favor by hiring him. Mom probably had a lot to do with that, convincing her husband to have mercy on her son. But if Dexter fired him, he'd have to find another job which might not be so easy for a felon. Riley exhaled a long breath.

"Look. I didn't put you on the calendar yet because we need to have a talk." The older man twirled a pencil between two fingers. "I've received some complaints from a couple of clients. If it were only one, I wouldn't worry so much, but three—Harbor Lights Office Building, Pacific Bank, and Woodlyn Realty. All three you serviced in the last month."

Okay, so he wasn't the most thorough janitor Dexter had on staff. Riley chewed on the edge of his pinky. "What kind of complaints?"

The other man pounded his fist on his desk. "Towel dispensers not refilled, half of the garbage pails not emptied, carpets not vacuumed. How's that for starters?"

Riley gulped. He couldn't argue with the guy. He tended to overlook things, and he had to admit, he slacked off too much of the time. Even as a kid, he'd procrastinate about raking leaves or cleaning his room when Mom asked him. When she finally yelled at him, he'd do a halfway job just to be finished. Same old thing now.

This wasn't the way to prove to Dex and Mom that he could accept responsibility for his life. He scooted farther down in his chair and studied the carpet. If he lifted his head, would Dexter hit him?

Dexter stuck a pencil behind his ear and peered at him. "Okay, buddy. I'm giving it to you straight. I offered you this job because your mom was afraid you'd wind up dealing drugs and find yourself in jail again. I'm doing her a favor, and you."

Back in jail? Riley shivered. God forbid. He didn't want to see the inside of that place ever again. "I…uh hmm…" He sat up straight. "The Lord came into my life while I was in prison. I'm not going to return to that hole."

Who knew if Dexter believed that or not? Maybe he'd even scoff at his remarks. But still, his boss had a valid complaint.

Riley's shoulders slumped forward. Though he had failed so many times before, he needed to finally get his life right. *God help me.*

"But you're still trying to take shortcuts, Riley." His stepfather placed his elbows on his desk and laced his fingers. "That's what got you into your mess in the first place. I can always tell when one of the foster kids will run into trouble. Your momma and I have taken in enough of 'em to see the signs." Dexter's piercing look made the muscles in Riley's jaw twitch.

The urge to tune out Dexter's words tempted him, like every time he'd received a rebuke. A cold chill rifled through him. He tapped his head with his fist. *What am I doing? The man is only stating facts. I can't avoid the truth any longer.*

His boss folded his hands over his chest. "You couldn't take the time to study when you were in college. You wanted money and girls. The drug dealing made you a big man—for a while, but look where you are now. This job may not be glamorous, but it's one you can be proud of. You can hold your head up if you'll put in an honest day's work. Do it right."

"I'll do better." Riley locked eyes with his stepfather. "I promise."

"All right. This is a trial period. I'll hold you to your word." Dexter flipped through the pages in a file folder next to the calculator. "Oh, yeah. We have a new account." He closed the folder and drummed his fingers on top. "Woodlyn Hospital."

A cold chill ran through Riley. Woodlyn Hospital.

Where Jillian worked. The last thing he wanted was for her to find out about his profession. *God, is this some kind of punishment?*

Dexter whipped a piece of paper toward him. "Here's your schedule. And listen. I don't mean to sound too harsh, but if I continue to get complaints, I don't care if you are my wife's son, you're out of here."

~

The woodland trail made a good place to think when he needed to. And pray. Riley ground his molars as he stepped out of his car in front of Evergreen Fellowship. His neck still burned after his talk with Dexter.

The chilly May afternoon cooled his face, and some of the embarrassment and disappointment slipped away. "But Dex had every right to scold me. I deserved it." *The shortcuts.* He couldn't argue about it. He fastened the top button on his jacket and shoved his hands into his pockets.

One glance at his watch told him he still had two hours before his shift at Woodlyn Hospital. He peered around the end of the red brick church. The yard in back was neatly mowed in straight rows with no missed patches and the grass trimmed around tree trunks. At least he'd done something right.

He stroked the stubble on his chin with two fingers. A kid throwing a pity party couldn't set a worse example. He needed to take ownership of his bad habits, but why was it so hard?

The sight of western Washington's towering Douglas fir and lush forests energized him. A contrast to the cement walls, concrete floors, and dirty jail cell where he often shivered on cold, rainy nights. Thank God those days were over.

Beyond the yard, the woodland trail meandered through a clearing. Dead leaves from last autumn lay crinkled and dry on the forest floor and moss-covered part of the ground. He reached down and picked up a brown, withered leaf. *When you were on the tree last year, I sat in a prison cell.* He tapped his fist on his forehead. Didn't do him any good to think like that.

An old rock wall, crumbling with age, emerged ahead. If the trees could talk, perhaps they'd tell of a homesteader who lived there long ago. Tales of the man's hopes and plans, his accomplishments and failures and perhaps the woman he loved.

The path split the wall where the stones had collapsed. Then the trail zigzagged through a stand of evergreens.

He hiked through the opening and settled on a downed log on the other side. With his hands covering his face, he tried to clear his mind of the way he'd messed up his life. "God, if it wasn't for You, I wouldn't have any hope at all. I wonder if I'll ever be at a point where I please You."

You please me now.

The words leapt through his mind. Had he thought them trying to make himself feel better?

The message the warden had spoken to him the day he walked out of prison filled his mind. He gripped his hand into a ball. Two out of three released inmates are rearrested within three years, the man had warned. Not only that, but sixty percent of all drug dealers lapsed back into old habits within the same three-year period.

He whispered to the pine trees. "Will I make it another two and a half years?"

He darted up and paced down the path toward the outcropping of trees. "God, I want to do the job right for Dexter, but I'm so used to taking shortcuts. Please, Lord, don't give up on me. Help me to remain accountable to You, to Dexter, to Mom, and to myself."

A picture of the blue-eyed doctor crossed his memory—her resolve to gain her credentials. It must have taken determination and hard work. Now, she assisted in bringing new life into the world. "Lord, for whatever reason You sent me to work at the hospital, I want to follow through and do the job you've given me to do. I trust in you, alone."

But trusting in God wasn't enough if he didn't allow HIm to work in his life. Would the stats win or could he give God the reins?

~

Jillian checked off her last patient on Monday's list and filed the schedule. All had showed—except one. Sorrow wrenched her heart, threatening her with unwanted tears.

Since Jamie hadn't paid Jillian a visit this afternoon, chances were slimmer she'd come at a later date, though Jillian could always hope. The poor misguided girl might make the same mistake she had. Jillian fought the despondency she endured so often.

If Jamie did seek the abortion, how would she fill her days afterwards? Better than Jillian had, she prayed.

The first week Jillian had concentrated on healing physically, thankful she lived in the dorm so her parents wouldn't find out. When she started back to class again, she buried herself in her studies, avoiding any thought of the procedure. But had she lost part of herself in the process?

Finally, a friend from college asked her to attend church, and Jillian gave her life to the Lord. As freeing as that was, she still didn't find release from her guilt.

Her cheeks warmed. If she were honest, she'd admit she'd continued to want a man's attention, the need the college man had filled that night months earlier. But she couldn't go about satisfying her longings the wrong way—hoping into bed again. She loved the Lord and couldn't go against his statutes.

Through her Bible studies, she learned that Christ died for all her mistakes, including her abortion. But she couldn't move past the culpability that hadn't given her peace in ten years. Did every Christian have a *dark side* they loathed, yet needed to face? She suspected most did. But her dark side—the ugly truth about her selfish decision to abort her own flesh and blood, seemed darker than anyone else's could possibly be. The father of her baby had behaved recklessly, but he didn't destroy his own child.

Mom. If she could hear her sweet voice for a minute, the unhappy feeling in Jillian's heart might go away. She fished for her cell in her coat pocket.

"Hello, Jillian. Your dad and I were just talking about you. We're going to hold you to that promise to visit at Christmastime."

Mom's voice soothed her like a cup of hot apple cider on a winter evening. "Hi." She hoped she didn't sound as downcast as she felt. "How's everything?"

"Oh, the flowers in my garden are all in bloom.

May is such a beautiful month in New York. But I have a feeling you didn't call to talk about the weather."

"Well, if you want to know the truth, I just needed to hear your voice. I guess I had a rough day."

"What happened?"

"Oh, a no-show patient, for one thing. I'd hoped to encourage her in her pregnancy. I'm afraid she's contemplating abortion now."

"Tell me her name, and I'll pray for her."

Jillian. She gasped. *Oh, where did that come from?* "Jamie."

"All right, honey. I'll keep her in prayer."

"I love you, Mom. Pray for me, too."

Jillian slid her phone back in her pocket, rested her head against her high-backed office chair, and closed her eyes. Her stomach tightened into a knot.

She could never tell Mom and Dad what she did ten years ago—not because they'd judge her, but because they'd grieve for their grandchild, for Jillian. She couldn't let them down like that.

Once again, a murky image meandered through her mind, a recollection of the young college student she'd gone too far with. His features were always obscured, but perhaps that was best. She didn't want to see him— the face of her baby's father. Her eyes stung, and she swiped at them. God would never allow her to have a baby now. She didn't deserve a family. Not after her careless and foolish actions.

JUNE FOSTER

Chapter Four

A safe arrival of another healthy baby. Jillian gave her patient a wave before she stepped into the hall from the hospital room. The wisp of red hair on the top of the baby girl's head made her laugh. And the baby had a little mouth shaped like a bow.

Joy bubbled up inside her. Another new life had entered the world. She unfastened the tie on her surgical scrub gown, slipped her arms out, and draped the garment over one arm.

A stern voice emanating from the nurses' station caught her attention.

Jett towered over the RN on duty, who looked up at him with wide eyes and nodded, obviously in awe of his reputation as one of the most skilled doctors on staff. Jett pointed toward the opposite hall.

The nurse picked up a manila folder and started in that direction.

Dr. Jett Camp could be a bit firm, but then his stringent standards made him a good doctor. Though he barked out his orders at times, he placed the welfare and care of his patients first, and Jillian admired him for that.

Jett. Their relationship had deepened in the last

year. At least she'd perceived it that way. After all, they'd spent almost every weekend together, made those trips to Seattle, Mt. Rainier, and even a weekend to the San Juan Islands. He'd wanted to get one room, but she'd insisted on two. She'd made a mistake in college and chose not to slip into a promiscuous lifestyle now, or ever. He hadn't objected to her request, for which she was glad.

But was Jett the person she wanted to spend her life with? He treated her with gentlemanly charm and wowed her with compliments, romantic dinners on the waterfront in Seattle, and gifts.

Woman's intuition informed her of a ring in her immediate future. Her pulse skipped a beat. She couldn't deny the doctor was handsome and eligible. Only one problem. He probably didn't support her dream of a clinic for pregnant teens—always changed the subject when she mentioned it. But she wouldn't concern herself about that. He'd catch her vision in time, once he knew more about her plans.

His abrasive voice alerted her again. With his hands folded over his white coat, Jett challenged another of the on-duty nurses behind the desk. "Mrs. Duncan, have you finished taking the health history of my patient in 205?"

She looked up, clasping her pen in one hand. "That's next after I finish my notes on 210."

A shiver traveled through Jillian. The woman must be new. None of the nurses responded to Jett like that. Most complied immediately.

"Mrs. Duncan. If you don't mind, I need the information before I can visit this patient and make a decision on her case."

The nurse raised an eyebrow and opened her mouth as if to speak but closed it again. She smiled, nodded, and picked up a clipboard, marching down the hall in the direction of 205.

The muscles in Jett's face relaxed as he fronted a glance at Jillian and sighed. "These nurses. Sometimes I feel like I have to prod them."

"Jett…" Jillian clamped her mouth shut. It wouldn't do any good to tell him to lighten up a little. At least he set a high standard, and the nurses knew they had to comply.

Dr. Bloomfield stuck his penlight into the pocket of his white jacket as he marched down the hall toward them. "Just the two people I need to speak with." A furrow marked his brow, and he pressed his lips into a tight line.

Jett lifted his chin. "What's going on, Eric?"

Perusing the clipboard in his hand, Eric blew out a breath of air. "I need to run a case by you and Jillian. One of my clinical patients."

Jillian checked her watch. "I've got a few minutes."

"Yeah, sure. Let's go to the conference room." Jett filed down the first corridor to the right then turned the corner and tried the door.

"Good, it's empty," Eric said. "Thanks, guys. I appreciate this."

The oval conference table could accommodate eight. Eric pulled out a chair at the far end and thumbed through his file.

"Here's the situation." He rubbed his brow with two fingers. "An ultrasound indicates the fetus has a birth defect. The back portion of the baby's skull hasn't developed and much of the brain is outside the head.

There's a three percent chance of survival. I can terminate the pregnancy now by injecting a needle into the heart."

A knife split Jillian's breastbone. Eric spoke the words like a television anchor reporting the news. If she looked at the man, he'd see the disbelief on her face. Though she'd been trained not to display her emotions in treating a patient, Jillian could never get used to the negatives that accompanied obstetrics.

"The other choice is delivery by C-section at term. I can take bone from the mother's hip to form the back of the baby's skull. But the portion of brain mass outside the head cannot be salvaged."

Though Jillian dealt with medical matters on a daily basis, when she allowed the reality to permeate her thinking, the idea of ending a baby's life with a needle lacerated her emotions. But an old voice sounded within her. Hadn't she permitted a doctor to rip her child from her uterus?

Jett folded his arms over his chest. "Look, Eric. All you can do is present the options to the parents."

"Yeah, that's why I wanted to talk to you both. I'm not sure if I can talk the parents out of the decision they've made."

Jett sniffed. "Which is?"

"They've chosen to keep the fetus full term." Eric shuffled another paper in the file and coughed. "There's nothing more I can say to them. They know the consequences. But they're some kind of religious fanatics. I really don't understand their thinking."

"I suppose they're allowing their misguided preconceptions to direct them." Jett tapped his pencil on the table.

Misguided preconceptions. What did he mean? Jillian bit her finger, restraining the words she wanted to blurt out. Was that a swing at the couple's faith? Surely not.

Jett knew her strong convictions and had never criticized her beliefs. She figured he held to the same faith she did. At least he'd talked about believing in God. Maybe she'd assumed too much. "Jett, the Almighty can deliver that child or take it, but it should be God's choice, not ours."

"Jillian, you're a doctor." Jett slid a pen behind his ear and shrugged. "You're supposed to make medical decisions with your knowledge of science, not with your sentiments." He twisted toward Eric. "Women doc..." He widened his eyes then snapped his mouth shut.

What had he almost said? Something derogatory about women doctors, no doubt. Now her blood pounded in her ears. Eric and Jett talked about this baby as if it were a thing instead of a person God created. The door to the consultation room slammed with a bang after she stormed out. She'd had enough.

Jillian keyed in the code to the doctor's lounge. Even the muted walls and low, contemporary furniture didn't soothe her irritation. She paced the empty room. "If only I'd realized the life of my baby was God's choice. God's choice, not mine." She brushed a tear away. Her anger turned to sorrow. Why couldn't people stop in the midst of their problems and allow God's solutions instead of their own faulty ones?

When another doctor walked in, she turned her back on the door. Allowing a co-worker to see her display of emotions wasn't wise. She had to maintain professionalism at the hospital.

Strong hands gripped both of her shoulders. "Jillian." Jett's whispered utterance comforted her.

She curved to face him.

"I'm...I'm sorry." He smiled and brushed a tear from her face. "My remark was uncalled for. I have the greatest respect for you and your ability as a doctor. You're right. The choice is subjective and ultimately should be made by the parents. I thought that..." He cracked his knuckles. "Jillian, you know you mean more to me than anyone or any medical case." He pulled her close to his chest and wrapped his arms around her.

His embrace melted her annoyance as she relaxed in his arms. She tightened her hands around his neck. Maybe she was wrong. When Jett criticized the family for not taking Eric's first option of ending the pregnancy, he merely questioned their decision in a medical sense. He hadn't disrespected their religious beliefs not to terminate the baby's life. Had he?

Now that she thought of it, she should've apologized to him instead of the other way around. Taking her angry feelings toward herself out on him wasn't fair. This disagreement was her fault, not Jett's.

"You have the most beautiful eyes." He nuzzled her cheek with his lips. "You know how I feel about you. How I have hopes for our future." He kissed her wet cheek, then the side of her mouth. "I'm thinking about us. I want more, much more."

Chapter Five

Mrs. Schmidt, her distended abdomen visible under the sheets, displayed a bright smile, followed by a grimace after Jillian tapped on her hospital door and stepped inside.

Swallowing hard, Mr. Schmidt sat at the edge of the upright chair next to his wife's bed. When he stroked her hand, he pasted on an artificial smile.

"Hello, you two. Looks like we're going to have a little baby pretty soon."

The mom-to-be blew out a breath and reached for Jillian's hand. "Dr. Coleman, I'm glad you're here. The nurse said the contractions are about six minutes apart."

Giving a patient less than positive news wasn't Jillian's favorite part of her job. "I've reviewed the ultrasound." She stiffened her shoulders and squeezed her patient's hand. "After my pelvic exam, I suspected the baby was breech. The Ultrasound has confirmed it."

Mrs. Schmidt clutched her throat. "How will that affect my delivery?"

"As I explained at our office visit a couple of weeks ago, breech babies are generally delivered by caesarean section." Jillian patted the patient's shoulder. "Since you're full term and your baby's weight is normal, you could deliver naturally, but only if she remains in complete breech where her legs are folded at the buttocks. If she shifts into footling breech, in other words, one of her feet are pointing down into the birth canal, then we'd have to take her by cesarean."

"I'm not sure." Mrs. Schmidt bit her upper lip.

Jillian squared her shoulders. "Don't worry. We have a doctor on staff, Jett Camp, who's trained in natural breech births. Or you could choose a C-section."

"What are the risks of a C-section?" She gave a quick glance at her husband.

"Well, for one, a C-section is surgery and would require a longer recovery time."

"Honey, what do you think?" A furrow appeared on Mr. Schmidt's face.

"Why don't you two discuss it for a moment?" Jillian curved toward the door. "I'm going to speak with Dr. Camp. We'll get his opinion, too."

"O…okay." Mrs. Schmidt grabbed her stomach and frowned. "Wait." She blew out three quick breaths. "Can't you do anything?" She huffed again. "*Ow.* This is getting uncomfortable." She rubbed her abdomen.

"Don't worry. Dr. Blakely will be in soon to start an epidural." Jillian gave her patient a smile over her shoulder and stepped into the hall. Though Jillian delivered babies every day, she trusted Jett's expertise with breech deliveries.

Another mother-to-be lumbered in slow motion down the hall, holding onto the railing with one hand and her stomach with the other. *She must be one of Eric's patients.*

The lady smiled at Jillian. "They're going to send me home if the contractions don't progress any faster."

Jillian nodded to her with a grin and pulled her cell phone out of her pocket. She typed in the text. *Jett, need to talk. ASAP.*

As she neared the long, curved desk, she circled around to Jett's masculine rumble behind her.

"Just finished with a patient. What's up?"

She exhaled a sigh, grateful he was available so soon. "I need your assistance. Mrs. Schmidt in 212 is complete breech. Her contractions are about five to six minutes apart. She may want to deliver vaginally rather than C-Section. Could you help me out and talk to her?

Jett winked. "Anything for you, gorgeous."

"Jett, get serious." Jillian clasped her hands behind her back.

"I'm on it." He headed toward 212. His flirty gesture was probably part of his campaign to treat her like a queen after their argument last week.

For a step or two, Jillian followed him, but snapped her fingers. Dr. Blakely. She needed to contact him. Since the nurses' desk was only steps away, she stopped. "Jett, I'll catch up with you in a minute," she called to the back of his head.

Mrs. Duncan hung up the phone and lifted a finger. "Dr. Coleman, excuse me."

"Yes, Ma'am," Jillian rested her elbows on the sleek white countertop.

"Your patient, Mrs. Tinley, has been admitted. She's in room 225. I believe her contractions started a few hours ago, and her placenta is still intact."

"Okay, thanks Mrs. Duncan. I'll check on her. Oh, can you notify Dr. Blakely Mrs. Schmidt in 212 is ready for an epidural?"

"Yes, doctor." Mrs. Duncan picked up the phone

again.

Jillian proceeded up the hall on the other end from Mrs. Schmidt's room. Jett could use a little time with her anyway. It wouldn't take long to make sure Mrs. Tinley's labor progressed normally.

A picture of the concern on Mrs. Schmidt's face sprang into her mind's eye. "Lord, please give us wisdom in delivering my patient's baby. Allow her child to arrive safely." She mumbled barely allowing her lips to move.

Room 225 appeared, and Jillian tapped at the door.

Mrs. Tinley lay in her bed, the fetal monitor attached.

"Hi, there." Jillian greeted her with what she hoped was a cheery smile. "I wanted to say hello and let you know I'm here on the floor. We'll be delivering your little one after a while."

Her patient's sparkling blue eyes twinkled. She ran a hand over her belly. "Oh, Dr. Coleman, my husband and I have been waiting for this day. Our own baby. You don't know how long we prayed for our son. And now he's finally arriving in the world." She laughed. "God is so good."

Mrs. Tinley's face told Jillian the whole story. God was indeed a miracle worker. The strong beeps of the fetal monitor confirmed the healthy baby's presence.

But she flinched. *Some mothers don't see their babies as a blessing, but a hindrance.* Hadn't that been her own point of view? *Oh God...* Jillian looked from Mrs. Tinley to the bright face of her husband hurrying from the hall into the hospital room. Would the day ever come when she could forgive herself?

"Okay, honey. All set. I made the calls." Mr. Tinley

smiled and grasped his wife's hand. "Everyone is praying for us."

"I'll be back to check on you later. Your son may not be here for a while. First babies take their time." She turned toward the door. "Congratulations, you two."

With a nod to Mrs. Duncan, Jillian ambled past the nurses' station toward Mrs. Schmidt's room. Jett poked his head out the door and took a few steps into the hall.

This time, his demeanor conveyed a more serious frame of mind. Lines creased his brow, and he lowered his voice. "I've talked to Mrs. Schmidt. I took another ultrasound and the fetus has shifted to footling breech. As you know, we can't do a vaginal breech birth unless the baby presents a complete breech, but I'm suggesting we give it awhile and see how the labor progresses. She was in complete before. The baby could move again." Jett stroked his chin. "And another issue. Seems the mother now refuses a C-section. By hospital policy, she has the right to do so. We can't go against her will."

A thought eroded Jillian's confidence. Though Jett had additional training in natural breech delivery, if the baby wasn't in complete, the child could be in danger as the labor progressed. Not to speak of the difficulty for the mother.

Jillian rubbed her forehead and set out toward the door to the hospital gardens. She needed a moment of fresh air. *Lord, give us wisdom.*

A concrete bench sat under the shade of a plum tree, its leaves a dark purple. She sank down onto the seat, breathing in the evergreen-scented spring air. Like the Tinley's, Mrs. Schmidt had mentioned at every appointment how she and her husband had awaited the arrival of their precious baby girl. *Was my baby a boy or a girl?* She bounded to her feet and paced.

An hour had passed since she'd first spoken to Mrs. Schmidt. Jillian followed the path out of the gardens, leaving the clean air of the out-of-doors for the sterile, hygienic smell of the hospital halls. Even before she entered room 212, she heard the groans.

Mrs. Duncan placed a blood pressure cuff on the patient. "Oh, Dr. Coleman. Dr. Blakely finished the epidural about five minutes ago."

The fetal monitor indicated the baby's heartbeat was normal. Maybe by now the infant had shifted to complete. Jillian would check again.

She tightened her jaws and removed her latex gloves. The baby was still in footling breech. Apprehension constricted her chest. To make matters worse, Mrs. Schmidt wasn't dilating.

Though Jett was an expert in his field, a premonition niggled her. She needed to get this baby out now. Jillian neared the front of the bed.

"Mrs. Schmidt, Dr. Camp mentioned that you'd rather not go the C-section route. I'd like you to reconsider. There are a couple of factors. You're not dilating properly." She gave a swift glance at the computer screen. "The baby's pulse has dropped a bit as well."

Jillian's patient squeezed her eyes shut. "Dr. Coleman, my husband and I have made our decision. We want the most natural approach."

Fear gurgled up from Jillian's abdomen. She needed to deliver this baby in the next half hour. She jerked her attention toward the monitor again. The baby's heart rate plunged even farther.

A doctor's professional decision always held an element of personal judgment. She weighed the odds—delaying delivery or proceeding now.

Though Jett wanted to see how the labor progressed, the medical conditions had changed. Jillian had to bring the baby into the world now.

"Please. Listen to me." The thought of any child dying needlessly shredded her emotions. "This baby needs to be born. I can't wait any longer. We could be risking the life of this child."

The patient gasped. "My baby...could die?"

Jillian didn't want to bring alarm to the parents, but they needed to know. She nodded praying her expression displayed the urgency. "Please...reconsider."

Mr. Schmidt stood. "Honey, we can't take any risks. Let's honor Dr. Coleman's recommendation." Thankfully the husband finally expressed his opinion.

The patient knit her eyebrows and turned to Jillian with eyes rimmed red. She moved her head up and down. "All right."

Thank God. Jillian pressed the nurse's call button. "This is Dr. Coleman. Send a couple of assistants to room 212. Let's get Mrs. Schmidt ready for a C-section."

Jillian turned back to her patient. "I'm going to OR to scrub now, Mrs. Schmidt." She grasped her hand and squeezed. "Everything's going to be fine."

A tear threatened, but she took a quick breath and stepped into the hall.

"Jillian, what do you think you're doing?" Jett paced toward her.

"Shh." She grasped his hand and led him down the

hall nearer the nurses' station. "This is my decision. Unless you want to deliver a dead baby." She gasped at the sound of her own words. "The heartbeat has steadily dropped. I can't wait any longer."

"I suppose you talked her into it." Jett's face hardened as the muscles in his face tightened.

Jillian's exasperation forced her breath into an unsteady rhythm impeding the flow of her words. "You're right, I did, Jett. She's my patient, and I've got the final say."

"You asked me for my advice and help." He folded his arms over this chest and raised his chin. "Next time maybe you should remember that you don't trust my opinion before you call me in on a case."

"Jett." Jillian's shoulders slumped. "Please support me."

"All right, I'll assist you in the delivery. But I still think we should wait."

~

Riley pushed the rolling utility cart out of the janitor's closet. Fresh soapy water sloshed in the bucket attached to the front. His bottles of cleaning liquids were stored in one of the bins on top. The paper towels, toilet paper, and soap dispenser refills lay in the larger cart below. Mops and brooms attached to the back next to the large waste receptacle.

At first when Dexter told him he'd have to work in hospital maintenance, temptation had nagged him. He wanted to say no and ask his stepfather to put someone else on the job. The idea that Jillian could see him in action, scrubbing floors, empting garbage, cleaning windows, and sanitizing bathrooms sent a surge of dread through him.

To add to his frustration, he'd lain in bed last night for hours daydreaming about the responsible, hardworking doctor. Jillian at the baby shower, Jillian on the jogging trail, Jillian ministering to that young pregnant teen. Why couldn't he be more like her?

The lovely doctor had no idea of his past, a lowly maintenance worker who'd spent ten years in prison. And before that, he wasn't much better—a young college student who took advantage of another. But if he encountered her, he'd deal with it. She'd find out eventually anyway. *Face it, Mathis, you'll never be in her league.*

Riley pushed the cart a few feet away from the closet and down the hall toward the nurses' station. He'd start in the main corridor.

"Jillian, I think you should reconsider." A gruff, masculine voice uttered the strong words.

The tall, blond man in a white medical jacket rushed alongside Jillian as they moved in Riley's direction. The name badge on the guy's coat said *Dr. Jett Camp.* The doctor took a few steps in front of her, blocking her progress down the hall.

Hmm. Dr. Jett Camp. Wasn't that the doctor he'd overheard the labor and delivery nurses talking about? The man who struck fear in their hearts?

"Jett, I know what I'm doing. I'm saving a child's life." She took a step to one side and raised her voice. "Move. We don't have any time to spare."

"All right, I'll assist you in the delivery. But I still think we should wait." Dr. Camp gave her a sneer.

Caught in the drama unfolding before him, Riley

stared. Jillian stormed toward him, her mouth pressed together in a straight line. She looked at him, but no expression of acknowledgement dawned on her face. With heavy steps, she marched down the hall in the direction of the OR sign. When she passed him, she stared through him like he was a ghost.

Mathis, you just can't get it through your head, can you? He brought his fist to his forehead with a tap. *Maybe now you will. You're a nobody, a low-life janitor with a prison record. Important people like doctors don't even know you exist. You're like the soap scum in your custodian's bucket.*

Chapter Six

Oh, dear Lord. It was close. Jillian stumbled out of the OR and ripped her mask off. She fought against her tears. Never had a baby's heart drop that low before delivery. *We almost lost her.*

The surface of the wall supported her weight. She might topple any moment. Slipping out of her latex gloves, she tossed them in the garbage receptacle near the door. She'd hoped, as Jett did, that they could wait for the baby to shift, but in the end she'd made the best decision.

The glad faces of the mother and father had been all the reward she needed. Jillian's heart twisted into a knot. Those two people would've been devastated and gone home childless if they'd delayed any longer.

Thank God the baby hadn't suffered any lasting effects from the ordeal. The beautiful little girl breathed well on her own, and her pressure returned to normal.

Jillian released a deep sigh and straightened. Standing out in the hall next to the OR blubbering like an idiot was ludicrous. Doctors should be more in control.

A man on his knees with his back to her scrubbed the tile with a large brush. His muscular shoulders visible through his brown janitor's shirt tensed and relaxed with every stroke. She'd never seen a custodian put so much effort into his work as he sank the bristles into the tiles.

He stood and pulled his mop from the back of his cart. With long swipes, he drew the sponge over the suds, and rinsed it in the clear water of his red plastic pail. When he glanced up, their eyes connected.

Riley? Her pulse jolted. Did he work…?

The door to the OR flew open, and Jett walked out. He removed his mask and shrugged his shoulders. Without slowing his pace, he whisked past her and lowered his voice. "A lucky call this time, Jillian."

Lucky call? How could he say that? A precious life had held in the balance.

Jillian's exhausted body folded into a chair at the end of the hall near the OR. The pent-up emotion wouldn't wait any longer. A baby had almost died today. Sobs shook her shoulders.

"What...what did you say to her?" A quiet masculine voice muttered. With a few steps forward, Riley peered at Jett. "I think you owe her an apology." He dropped his gaze to the floor.

"What the…" Jett drew his fist in front of him.

In disbelief, Jillian stood transfixed.

Jett glared at Riley, tapping his chest over and over. "Who do you think you are, you lowlife?"

She bit her lip and rushed to them, grasping Jett's arm. This couldn't be happening.

With an easy push, Jett brushed her away. He curled his lip and grabbed the front of Riley's shirt with both hands and shook him. "This is none of your business." He released Riley, placed his palms on his chest, and shoved him hard.

When Riley lost his footing on the wet floor, he stumbled backward and landed on his rear-end. Scrambling to his feet, he glanced back at the area he'd cleaned. He shook his head. "And I deserve to be fired. I'm sorry."

"Riley, wait." Jillian took a few steps toward the men again. "Jett, calm down."

She worked her way between Jett and Riley. Jett glared at the janitor who hung his head like a bad dog. "Why did you say that to Dr. Camp?"

"I...I thought he said something that upset you." Riley lifted tortured eyes. "Your face paled."

Riley must've thought Jett spoke an offensive word to her. Her heart softened. He had only wanted to shield her from pain, to protect her. Compassion for the man, even concern, built in her. The sweet guy thought he was doing the right thing.

Jett held two fists in front of his chest, still on guard.

"Riley is a friend." She blew out a breath." I'd appreciate it if you didn't make an issue of it. He misunderstood the situation."

But had Riley actually misunderstood Jett's intensions? What Jett said had hurt her. *A lucky call.*

"A friend?" Jett shrugged. "Yeah, whatever." He pressed past her. "Forget it. I wouldn't want to see his minimum wage check yanked away."

Jillian's mouth fell open. She'd never heard Jett speak in such a condescending manner.

Riley thrust his hands in his pockets and peered from Jett to her. "Thank you." He crept toward his cart.

She could no longer watch Riley as he progressed

farther down the hall. Heat filled her face. In many ways, he behaved in a more mature manner than Jett, though the doctor was an accomplished professional.

If Jillian thought her emotions wore her down earlier, they crushed her now. "Riley, come back, please." Did she imagine he shook his head? He continued on, not looking around, as if she'd never said a word.

Chapter Seven

The woman pushed out of the double doors of Woodlyn Hospital's spacious, all-purpose conference room. If Jillian hurried, she could catch up to her.

The bright sunlight warmed Jillian's face. She extended her hand and waved. "Mrs. Kennan, wait a second."

The middle-aged lady with soft brown hair curved around with a smile. "Yes, ma'am?" She paused on the sidewalk.

A few more steps and Jillian stopped in front of her. "I was impressed by your presentation to the group today. I believe you've provided foster care longer than any of the others who spoke."

The corners of her mouth lifted into a beam. "It's going on ten years now."

"Forgive me." Jillian stuck out her hand. "I'm Dr. Jillian Coleman. I attended the informational meeting to learn more about the foster care system. The health care program for these kids alone is a godsend, I'm sure."

Mrs. Kennan gave Jillian's hand a firm shake. "Yes, my little ones get stuffy noses and sick stomachs like any other kids. I'm blessed the state provides these resources."

"I'd like to make an in-home visit soon, to observe your program in action." Jillian shifted her purse to her other shoulder. "I'm planning to start a free clinic for teen girls contemplating abortion." Merely saying the words propelled her one step further toward her goal. "One service I'd like to provide, Mrs. Kennan, is arrangement for adoption if the mother so desires. I'd need foster care for the infant in some cases until the legal issues are resolved."

"Please, call me Marion." Mrs. Kennan's smile lit her face. "I'd be more than happy for you to visit. You'd get an idea of our routine and what a foster care home environment looks like." She squared her shoulders. "We could discuss some of those legal questions if you'd like."

"Thank you, Marion." Jillian pulled her card out of her pocket and passed it to the lady. "This means so much to me."

"Yes, and here's mine as well." Marion slipped her a card with the official DSHS logo. "I'll be looking forward to meeting with you soon." She waved and stepped off the sidewalk toward the parking lot.

Mrs. Keenan appeared to have it all together. A motherly woman. So suited for her job. Jillian clicked the locks of her Lexus and slipped into the driver's seat.

When her purse buzzed, she reached for her phone in the flap on her bag. She didn't have any patients nearing their due dates. *Hmm. Jett.* After his bad-mannered performance yesterday toward Riley, she was still fuming. *I'm not so sure I want to talk to him...Oh, well.* She'd see what he had to say. "Hello."

"Hello to the prettiest lady I know." His smooth masculine voice had lost its overbearing tone.

"Sounds like you're in a better mood." She hadn't intended to clip her words.

"I need to apologize for yesterday. I guess I was tired, as I'm sure you were. But that's no excuse." He produced a high-pitched laugh. "I reacted badly after the surgery—went a little overboard."

Overboard? So Jett's reaction didn't exhibit his actual opinion of Riley then, demeaning him as he did. "Riley Mathis probably thought you went more than a little overboard."

He snickered. "You're not really concerned about that janitor, are you?"

Jillian pulled the phone from her head and stared at it before listening again. Jett must be joking. "He goes to my church. He's a friend."

"Oh, that's right. I'd forgotten. Sorry. Your church—it's pretty important to you."

Surely his tone hadn't held the ounce of skepticism she imagined. "Not the church, Jett, but…" Jillian closed her eyes and pinched the bridge of her nose. She couldn't explain her relationship with Jesus Christ right now, though she should have months ago. Now that she thought of it, they hadn't talked about the matter at all.

"Hey, beautiful. Let's drop the subject of maintenance workers and church. I want to speak to you about something a lot more appealing. The Space Needle. Could I take you Saturday night?" He chuckled. "I have something of the utmost importance to talk about."

The Space Needle typified one of Seattle's most elegant restaurants with its circular view of the city and Elliot Bay—a grand location to give her a ring. Jillian scratched her head. This could be the proposal she'd expected.

A rising tide of excitement filled her chest. A diamond ring. She took a deep breath. "Yes, that sounds like fun."

She'd contemplated for months what marriage to Jett Camp would mean. She could quit her job at the hospital and work full time on setting up her clinic. One major advantage of marrying such a well established doctor. He made plenty of money for the both of them.

Yet, one thought worried her. What about his status with the Lord? Surely he believed as she. She'd bring it up first chance she had.

As if a pin pricked her, she released a long sigh. Another matter bothered her. Jett had ignored her every time she mentioned a free clinic. Would he support her in it? Jillian smiled. In time, she could convince him.

~

Five hundred feet above Elliot Bay, the view seemed more like a photograph. Jillian removed her white cloth napkin from her lap and placed it on the small table butted against the clear glass. Once more she glanced out the window. Snowcapped Mt. Rainier emerged, jutting up off the horizon. The panoramic view of Seattle from the Space Needle sent chills along her arms.

Across the table, Jett, his blond hair combed back off his forehead, watched her with twinkling blue eyes, as if he knew a secret.

She placed her hand on the wall next to their table. In only seconds, she drew it back as the table moved forward. She giggled. "I can't wrap my mind around the idea that we're moving, not the outside of the Space Needle."

Jett inched his hand from the dessert cup with remains of his crème briolette and slipped his fingers over hers. "I'm not looking at the Seattle skyline, Jillian. There's a better view right in front of me." He searched her face. "You're smart and beautiful, an astute, successful doctor..." He whispered. "... all I could ever want."

All he could want? What about what she wanted? But Jett didn't think that way. She knew he hadn't intended to sound selfish. The good-looking doctor's primary focus centered on bettering himself in his personal life and his career, for which she couldn't fault him.

Weren't his words a compliment? She'd captured the heart of this gorgeous, affluent doctor. What woman wouldn't want the attention of a professional career-man like Jett? She stole a glance at their entwined hands. "You flatter me."

With her free hand she ran her finger down the velvety petal of one of the red roses in a crystal vase on the table. Jett must've ordered them earlier in the day and had them delivered to the table. "And thank you again for the exquisite roses."

"There's a reason they're here." He gazed at their two hands, then lifted his eyes. "To get you in the mood."

Another hint she could only take one way. In a moment he would reach into his suit pocket and produce a little box. He'd snap it open and watch for the expression on her face.

Would the guy ever ask the question? She caught

her breath. How many carats would her diamond have?

"Jillian." Jett held her hand now with both of his. "Up here at the top of the world, I'd like to ask you if you'd do me the honor of becoming my wife." He paused, waiting for an answer.

"To marry you?" She scrunched her nose. *Where was the ring?*

Jett's hands hadn't released hers. As if he'd read her thoughts, he displayed a shy grin. "I...don't have the ring quite yet."

More like he doesn't want to make the investment until I say yes. "You can't expect me to answer you... without a ring." She wouldn't allow him to get away with this shabby treatment.

His smile faded to a pout. "Aren't you nit-picking a little?"

No, she wasn't quibbling, just holding him to a higher standard. But the evening couldn't end with a feud. Jillian batted her eyes a couple of times. "You've got to realize we females are sticklers for romance, which includes a dazzling diamond."

"Women," he muttered. He allowed a slow grin. "You're right." Glancing around, he lifted his hand to the waiter. "Check, please."

When the young man brought the bill on a black plastic tray, Jett signed it and dropped the pen. "The kid should be impressed with his tip." Jett smirked and puffed his chest out.

The server picked up the tray and his eyes widened. "Thank you, sir. Very much."

Jett either gave the kid a large tip because he cared or because he was trying to impress her. She shrugged.

Shoulders back and chin held high, Jett rose and

moved behind Jillian's chair. His warm breath tickled when he whispered in her ear. "You'll see a ring soon." He slid her chair back. "Ready?"

The guy could be charming, no doubt. "Can't forget these." She leaned toward the table and grasped the vase of roses before stealing one more look at the skyline. The lights of Seattle were more visible now, twinkling under the darkening sky over Puget Sound.

When they reached the edge of the revolving circle of tables, Jett grasped her elbow as they stepped onto the stationary platform. Several couples waited in the area with the long benches along the wall near the elevators.

A familiar woman sat next to a fifty-something man in slacks and a dress shirt. After a second glance, Jillian smiled at the plump lady. "Hi, Marion. How are you?"

The foster parent glanced up with a wide grin. "Hello, Dr. Coleman." She turned to a man with salt and pepper hair. "This is my husband Dexter Kennan."

Mr. Kennan stood and shook her hand then shot a glance at the man beside Jillian.

Jillian held her palm out toward Jett. "My friend Dr. Camp. Jett, Marion Kennan provides foster care in her home. I met her at a meeting at the hospital."

Jett shook hands with Mr. Kennan and nodded to Marion, a smile absent from his face. What was it about this innocuous couple that he didn't approve of?

"Dr. Coleman is an obstetrician at Woodlyn Hospital." Marion smiled at her husband and turned back to Jillian. "My husband's company recently got the maintenance contract for the hospital. My son, Riley Mathis, works there, now." She raised her chin and gave Jillian a bright smile. "He's trying to earn enough money to go back to college full time."

Her son? Jillian gaped at the smiling woman. Riley was her son? Why were their last names different?

"Riley." Jett curled his lip. "Isn't he the angry janitor who attacked me for no reason outside the OR when he stuck his nose in my face?"

Jillian chewed the inside of her cheek. That wasn't even close to the truth. Riley hadn't attacked Jett. Her grumpy doctor friend still didn't understand the situation.

"What?" Dexter's eyes grew large. "He what?" Marion's husband shook his head. "Wait a minute. Riley has got some problems, Dr. Camp, but anger isn't one of them. I'm sure there's got to be some other explanation." He swallowed hard.

"I hope you're not calling my integrity into question." Jett lifted his chin.

"Remember." Jillian ran her hand along Jett's arm. "I told you. Riley acted out of concern for me." She turned to Mr. Kennan, maintaining eye contact. "Please believe me. His actions were honorable. He meant no harm to anyone." She looked back at Jett, her shoulders tense.

Folding his arms over his chest, Jett stared above her, his mouth pinched into a tight line. Did he believe anything she said?

Marion and Dexter peered from her, to Jett, and finally toward the hostess station.

Surely Mr. Kennan understood. She prayed Riley wouldn't get into some kind of trouble as a result. She shifted from one foot to the other. "Well, uh… Marion, I'll call you in the next couple of weeks about making a home visit. I'm sure I'll gain invaluable information for when I need to make referrals for my adopted babies, once I get the clinic up and running."

"Kennan, party of two." The hostess held two menus in her hand.

"That's fine, Dr. Coleman. Call me when you're ready." Marion grasped her husband's hand and grinned. "We're celebrating our fourteenth wedding anniversary tonight."

Now Jillian got it. Dexter wasn't Riley's father. "Happy anniversary, you two. I'd recommend the beef Wellington. It's delicious."

Marion offered her one more smile as she and her husband followed the hostess up the revolving platform.

The elevator doors opened and Jett stood back, allowing her to enter first. His silence chilled her as the high-speed glass car descended the five hundred feet to the bottom. As the doors finally slid open again, they stepped out into the cool evening air of downtown Seattle.

Jett took a few strides next to her before he froze in the middle of the sidewalk, glaring at her. "Seriously, Jillian. You'd throw away all your education to open a clinic where you probably would never earn what we're worth? And what's up with you taking that janitor's side?"

JUNE FOSTER

Chapter Eight

Monday morning. Dexter would have Riley's schedule up this time. He trudged through the front door to Woodlyn Maintenance.

Not running into Jillian yesterday at church was a relief. Maybe she'd attended but he didn't see her. Or she could've had a delivery at the hospital. He didn't know. Anyway, after that embarrassing incident with Dr. Camp last week, he hoped he never saw her again, though a vague stirring within relayed a different message.

When was he going to stop dreaming about Jillian Coleman? Dreaming. A good description, like those wish lists people tend to make but never have any hope of obtaining. A fairytale that's nice to contemplate but never comes true.

His heart warmed. She'd stood up for him in front of the arrogant Doctor Camp at the hospital. *But maybe she just feels sorry for me.*

The familiar odor of disinfectant drew him back to his step-dad's office, Woodlyn Maintenance. He sniffed and covered his mouth for a sneeze. The bulletin board next to Dexter's office displayed his name about halfway down. *Okay, good.* He blew out a huff of air through puckered lips. His assignment was Woodlyn Hospital again. Maybe he should ask Dexter to switch him.

He tapped on his boss's office door and turned the knob.

Dex, with a pencil behind one ear, bent over some papers on his desk.

He must be crunching numbers again.

"Oh, Riley, come in. I need to talk to you." He pulled the pencil from behind his ear and scribbled something.

What now? Did Dr. Camp call and complain about him? "Yeah?" He pushed the door shut and edged down into the chair in front of his stepfather's desk.

As if a weightlifting inmate came at him with his fists, dread assaulted his stomach. The guy didn't even have the beginnings of a smile on his face. Dex was canning him this time. But why was his name still on the schedule?

His boss looked up from his seat on the other side of the gunmetal-gray desk and caught Riley's gape. "Your mom and I met Dr. Camp Saturday night at the Space Needle." He placed the pencil on the desk. "He was there with that lady doctor. I think you know her, Jillian Coleman."

What? Jillian out with that jerk? Riley's heart dropped into his shoes. Well, what did he expect? He could never afford to take her anywhere like the Space Needle. Besides, she wouldn't go out with the guy who cleaned the floors at the hospital. Especially if she remembered him and that night... His hand over his mouth didn't stifle the choking cough in his throat.

Dexter peered at him. "Doctor Camp told us how

you invaded his space and falsely accused him for no reason the other day in front of the OR at the hospital." Dexter challenged Riley with his stare as if waiting for him to say something.

What good would it do to defend himself? Riley had been in the wrong. Janitors don't go up to doctors and speak the way he did. "I suppose you want an explanation. I thought Camp had done something to hurt Jillian…I mean Dr. Coleman. It was all a misunderstanding. I overreacted. I'm sorry."

"The way your eyes lit up when you said Jillian…" Dexter cocked his head to the side as if trying to read Riley's thoughts. "I hope you're not…"

What does Dexter mean? I hope you're not what? Falling for the woman? Dexter knew as well as Riley he'd only suffer if he did.

His stepdad shuffled through the papers on his desk again. "You could've gotten me into a lot of trouble. We might have lost the contract."

"I'm sorry." Riley's thumbs twirled in front of him. His stepdad's rebuke hurt. But more than that, Jillian's betrayal stung even more. She hadn't stood up for him, telling Dexter and Mom what really happened. Guess she didn't think his minimum wage paycheck was worth protecting. "You said this was a trial period. I failed. I'll go pack up the things in my locker." He pushed up from the chair.

The silence sounded louder than if Dexter had yelled.

He rounded the desk and placed a fatherly hand on his shoulder. "Son, you're not fired. In fact, that pretty little doctor practically beamed when she excused your actions and told me they were honorable. I'm proud of you." He gave Riley a nudge in the ribs. "I probably wouldn't feel this way if I hadn't met the other doctor myself, but he is a first-class jerk."

The pretty doctor defended him? Riley's laugh filled the air, along with Dexter's loud guffaw. "I'll make sure that doesn't happen again, but when I saw her face, the hurt, I lost all reason."

"I've been up to the hospital a couple of times and noticed the work you've been doing recently." Dexter slapped his back. "You're putting more effort into your job."

Pride rose in Riley's chest. At this moment Dexter felt more like the dad he'd missed out on during his teens. He circled toward the door. With his hand on the knob, he looked back. "I've been thinking about taking some aggressive steps toward my schooling. This one class at a time when I could do more—well, it's another one of those shortcuts you pointed out, a half-hearted attempt to reach my goal, if you want to know the truth. When would it be best for me to sign up for classes? Would you rather I work days or nights?"

"How about working nights so you can go to class in the day?" Dexter's face brightened in a smile. "Also, let me give you the option. I can place you at another facility if you'd be more comfortable. Or you can remain at the hospital. The choice is yours."

If Riley went to another building, it would be running from his problems as he'd always done in the past, taking the shortcut, instead of facing his troubles straight on. "I'll stay at the hospital. If I can't deal with the pressure, then I'm not much of an employee."

Dexter cupped his hand to the side of his mouth like he knew a secret. "Hey, Riley. If you ask me, I think the doctor lady likes you. You couldn't do much better."

"Yeah, but she could." Riley pulled the door open and stepped out.

~

Riley stroked his chin. Since summer classes began in a few weeks, he needed to start thinking about financial aid. His car remained parked between Tim's and the church bus. He slid in and glanced at the brochures he'd picked up at the community college. For the summer session, he had enough from his savings, but the fall was another matter. If he didn't get funding, he might not be able to continue his classes.

For once the ignition started after he stuck his key in. His Google search last week for student loans revealed news he'd expected. Felons had a rougher time than others because few federal grants were available for convicts with a record of substance abuse, possession or selling. Thankfully, he'd identified a Christian organization that offered a grant to ex-cons. He'd found a couple of other private sources, too.

Riley rolled down his window and waved at Tim Garrett coming out of the church."Hey, Tim. Enjoyed the missions meeting. I'm anxious to get started."

"Yeah, dude. I'll let you guys know pretty soon, but I think we'll start with the Cascade Waterfall Park outreach since so many teens hang out there. Unfortunately, that's the central location of many of the drug deals going on in Woodlyn."

Tim didn't have to tell him that. How many times in the past had he made contact with vulnerable, naive teens as he sold his wares? Riley's face grew hot. The pain of regret speared him, wounding him worse than if Tim had run him through with a knife. He didn't deserve to be on the ministry committee, yet if he knew nothing else, he had assurance God had forgiven him. *Lord, this is my chance to give back some of what I took from those youths.* "Thanks for giving me this opportunity. Between this, my classes at the community college, and my job, I'm going to stay busy."

Tim gave him a knuckle-fist on his shoulder through the open window. "Don't forget what I said. When you come in to my office, you can talk about anything. I'm not here to judge you."

"I know." No doubt, his friend meant what he said from his kind eyes and easy smile.

"Okay." Tim tapped the roof. " See you next Sunday."

It must be nice. Tim had his life all together. A pretty wife and new baby on the way. He probably never had to deal with any tough issues in his past.

Riley slapped a palm on the steering wheel. He couldn't compare himself to anyone else. Of one thing he was sure. God loved him individually. That single truth saw him through those last miserable years in prison.

He gripped the steering wheel's leather cover. It would've been nice to talk to Jillian on the way out of the meeting, but he didn't bother her because she'd been busy with Tammy. Plus he felt like a bumbling school kid. Anyway, he was pleased she had a heart for missions.

When he put his Chevy in *drive,* he froze. Jillian emerged from the front door and headed toward her car in the side parking lot. She paused and turned in the opposite direction past the front door again and around to the back of the church. Maybe toward the Woodland Trail?

She disappeared around the corner of the building.

On impulse, he turned off the motor and stepped out. He didn't want to startle her, but he'd appreciate a chance to thank her for standing up for him in front of Mom, Dexter, and Dr. Camp. He traced her steps around the building and past the church lawn toward the trail.

Jillian poked along the path toward the rock wall, her hands clasped behind her. What was she thinking?

"Hey, Jillian." Whistling "Amazing Grace" as loud as he could, he narrowed the distance between them.

She stopped and rotated toward him, her mouth curved up at the edges.

Good. I didn't scare her.

Jillian's jeans and light-blue tee shirt hugged her curves, a contrast to her official lab coat that transformed her into the image of a successful doctor. "Hey, Riley. I thought I recognized your voice."

"Yeah." He caught up to her and returned her grin. "I wanted to talk to you. Uh…thanks for sticking up for me the other day at the Space Needle. Dexter told me about what you said."

"The Space Needle? Oh, yeah." Her face turned a pale pink. "I…um…I'm sorry for the whole misunderstanding. Doctor Camp can be a bit impulsive at times."

She took a few hesitant steps toward the broken wall and paused. Her smile faded as if a heavy weight had settled on her shoulders. With a tap of her tennis shoe, she knocked a rock out of the path on the moss-covered ground. Her eyes glistened with tears.

His pulse throbbed in his temples as he fought his urge to take her in his arms, to comfort her. Had Dr. Camp upset her again? "Jillian?"

"I...I'm sorry. I can't get Jamie out of my mind." She shook her head and long brown strands caught the breeze. "I know Tim said the focus of our outreach would be toward teens and drugs, but I pray we can contact some of the girls, like Jamie, who are contemplating abortion. I pray Jamie doesn't decide to kill her child." She circled toward the trees.

Riley reached for her arms and drew her around to face him. Tears rolled down her cheeks. He slid his hands from her shoulders, missing the warmth of her skin, and grasped his fingers behind his back, using all his will power not to embrace her. "We'll ask the Lord to put some of those girls in our path when we go out to the park. Like last time."

"Your faith in God, your tenderness toward the ministry is clear." Jillian lifted her long, wet lashes. "I look up to you for that."

Dr. Coleman respected him? "I could say the same thing to you. I suppose being a doctor who delivers babies...in your profession...you're more aware of the life a mother carries. I mean, with all the technology..."

"You believe my views are swayed because I'm an obstetrician? Maybe." She covered her face with both hands and turned her back to him again. "There's another reason, Riley."

She squared her shoulders and moved around to face him. "Somehow I feel I can share this." Her voice was barely louder than the leaves rustling with the gentle breeze. "You don't know how much I need to talk about my past with someone. It's a burden that almost crushes me sometimes. Maybe you could pray for me."

What heavy burden? Riley furrowed his brow. What did Jillian mean?

"Once...when I was in college..." She gulped as if she couldn't find the words. "I did something I have regretted, even until today." Her inhaled breath sounded like a sob. "I know God has forgiven me, but..."

A bitter chill crept along the muscles in Riley's back to his legs causing him to quiver. He knew what she was going to tell him. She'd slept with a man and now regretted it.

"I need to share this. I've told very few people." She grasped Riley's arm and squeezed. "In college...I usually didn't drink, but one night I did...way too many bottles of beer." She peered at something over his shoulder.

Jillian paused so long, Riley figured that's all she intended to say. But she locked her eyes on him. "Two of my girlfriends...They decided to stop at a fraternity party. They insisted I studied too hard and needed to get out. After we had a few more beers, I went upstairs with one of the frat guys." She enunciated each word as if voicing it brought her pain. "I was so far gone. I can't even remember what he looked like." Her shoulders shook with her sobs. "It only happened once. And after that—Riley, I've never slept with a man since."

Riley grasped her arm and ran his fingers down her delicate skin. "God can forgive you. He's a loving, merciful God." Hot fire flamed his neck. What kind of hypocrite was he? God could forgive her? He held as much guilt as she, if not more.

Now her voice became harsh and shrill. "Yeah, but can He forgive what I did a couple of months later—taking the life of the child I conceived that night?"

Air would not flow through Riley's lungs. He held his breath. *The child she conceived.* Her only time?

He knew all these years what he'd taken from her, but this?

"Please don't look at me with such condemnation." She dabbed at a tear on her cheek. "I aborted my baby, Riley. I can't live with the thought. Even after ten years." Her shoulders shook uncontrollably.

The truth penetrated him like shards of glass slicing him open. Jillian's baby. The baby was his, too. *Dear God.*

"I'm not criticizing you. God forbid. I've made so many mistakes in my life. I would never judge you." Even with that, he spoke the words of a charlatan. To beg for her forgiveness and God's…Would that be enough?

He drew her into his arms and closed his eyes. Her silky hair exuded the fragrance of fresh peaches. Riley swallowed a gulp. The mother of his child leaned against his chest.

Their offspring now lived with the Lord. Like the cold showers he took in prison, a notion chilled him. He couldn't tell her. *Dear God, I can't tell her.*

Another cool breeze shuffled the leaves again. Jillian's shoulders relaxed and she moved a step away from him.

He brushed her wet cheek with an awkward finger. Her lovely face set his heart pounding harder than before.

"I don't know why I told you. But somehow I feel

better, allowing someone else to help me carry the load." She squeezed her eyes shut. "I don't know what you must think of me now."

"Look at me, Jillian." Riley grasped her shoulders and lifted her chin with his finger. "If I judged you, I'd be a fraud. I want to carry the weight with you." But he knew he was a fake, keeping the truth from her.

"It was before I knew the Lord." She covered her eyes.

Gall rose in his throat. He allowed her to humble herself before him as if he had no responsibility in the matter. "We both did things we were ashamed of before we came to the Lord." He kicked at a downed evergreen branch at his feet. He could tell her part of the truth. Perhaps she'd be encouraged knowing she wasn't the only one who'd messed up their life.

"I was ashamed to tell you, but somehow, I feel free now." He held her hand against his chest as if that would make his story easier to hear. "There was a time in my life when I took drugs and sold them, an addict and a dealer. I spent ten years in prison for my crime." He blinked, waiting for her look of horror.

Her expression didn't change, and she squeezed his hand.

Riley peered deeply into her eyes. "When you think of it, a wrong is a wrong in God's eyes, none worse than another. Each one is a disgrace toward God. I thank Him for His mercy."

A smile sprang to her lips. "I don't think any less of you, Riley. You're right. Our mistakes are all equal in God's sight. Though we've been forgiven, I wish I could put mine behind me. Maybe someday." As if she'd journeyed to that *someday* in her mind, she peered beyond him.

"Thank you for not walking away from me in disgust." He smothered the urge to hold her again.

"I could never do that." Taking a few steps on the trail towards the church, she folded her hands behind her. "What are your plans for the future? You said you were taking online classes."

"I recently finished one, but I'm enrolled with a full load this summer." Riley caught up with her and kept pace by her side. "It's been my dream to become an accountant. If I can work hard, I should be done in three years with the extra classes I've taken and a couple I completed in prison."

Jillian smiled at him. "Well, you know, nonprofit clinics could use the sound advice of a financial advisor, especially with regard to tax issues."

For the first time, Riley envisioned God's plan, to work with Christian organizations. Jillian's words helped solidify it in his mind.

"The past needs to stay buried." She stopped and grasped his hand. "Look in the direction the Lord is leading you."

Riley gripped her hand harder. "You're right, but it's hard to ignore my mistakes. I've hurt so many people in the past. I'm afraid I could never do enough to regain their trust."

Chapter Nine

A parking place on the street in front of the park—unheard of. Riley backed in and pulled forward between a truck and a van. He dared a glance at the woman in the passenger's seat next to him. She was still there. Jillian Coleman hadn't vaporized. He wasn't dreaming.

Did Tim have a purpose when he paired the two of them at the missions meeting? Since the counselor had read the assignments from a printed copy, he must've decided earlier when he made his plans for the project. Riley trusted Tim's wisdom but still felt shy about partnering with an accomplished doctor.

After he hopped out, Riley raced around the front of the car to open the door, offering his hand. Jillian took it and stepped onto the curb.

He'd held her hand last Sunday afternoon on the woodland trail, the day that changed his life. He'd repeated the words over and over, trying to allow their meaning to seep into his soul. Jillian had conceived a baby that night ten years ago, his child. And he'd never known.

The truth was hard to bear. He'd missed out on the precious moments of fatherhood, holding his child in his arms and perhaps rocking the little one to sleep. A shiver cut a path through his chest.

Letting go of her hand, he gazed at her tee shirt with *Just Say No To Evolution* on the front. "Hey, Jillian, you want to pray again? I'm feeling a little nervous."

Sure, insecurity about their mission at the park niggled him. But he couldn't tell her the other reason his stomach clinched, more than when Dexter threatened to fire him. Learning he'd fathered a baby who now lived with the Savior was almost more than he could take in.

"I agree. Praying with the group didn't seem enough."

"Over here." Riley pointed to a tree across the path. Jillian followed him, and he turned to her.

She bit her lip. Now, she was a different Jillian than the Dr. Coleman from the hospital.

Her hands fit so well in his as he bowed his head. "Lord, we want to serve You today. Please put the young people in our path You want us to reach."

"Allow us to make a difference in Your kingdom." Jillian's words were little more than a whisper. "In Jesus name. Amen." She tucked a tendril of hair behind her ears. "You've got a heart for these kids. I can tell."

He nodded. "As do you. I think Tim said to begin there." Riley pointed in the direction of the commons and waved at two other team members strolling down the path, probably feeling as insecure as he and Jillian. Maybe after a few times, they'd become more bold.

Jillian put a hand on his arm. "My stomach is churning. I've never spoken to teens about drug use before."

"My hands are getting sweaty, too. This is a first for me. I'm hoping Tim's ministry teachings will kick in. I think God will use us if we're willing."

"I'm so glad Tim put me with you." She grinned. "You seem less intimidated."

Though she was probably unaware of it, her scrutiny made him nervous. He didn't deserve any of her praise. "I don't know about that. But I think God allows us to help people in areas where we've had a little experience." He snickered. "I spent ten years in jail for that crime. I want to warn others against the trap that put me there in the first place. I think the realization helps me to overcome my inhibitions."

They strolled down the path a short way. Jillian pulled a New Testament out of her pocket. "Only God could've changed a person the way He did you."

Riley lowered his gaze from Jillian's intense aquamarine eyes and examined an evergreen bush beside the path. "You're right. God did a work in me. I'd probably be dealing drugs in the park today and spending more time in prison if it wasn't for the Lord."

Two teenage boys in jeans, one wearing a cap perched on his head, the other with a hoodie, leaned up against a tree to their left. Both stared off toward the center of the park with empty, cheerless eyes. They were hungry for something more in their lives, but not the Lord. He knew. He'd been there. He glanced at Jillian, and her expression answered his unspoken question.

Lord, this is Your business. His heart pounded a little harder when he neared the teens, Jillian following him. "Hey, guys. How's it going?"

The kid with stringy brown hair that stuck out from under a Mariner's cap looked at Riley's tee shirt with *The Lord is My Shepherd* and scowled. "What are you, some kind of religious freaks trying to save us?"

Why did people always think of Christians as religious nuts? Riley scratched his head and prayed the teen would see his sincerity. "No, man. We just wanted to share with you how God made a difference in our lives."

"Look, I'm not interested in getting pure or holy. You're all a bunch of hypocrites." He repositioned his cap and stomped off down the path.

The other boy, so thin he looked like he'd never eaten a good meal, studied his Nike tennis shoes, then braced one foot on the tree trunk. "Yeah, my buddy doesn't like other people telling him what to do. His parents are real religious. They're always trying to force him to go to some church that tells the people you're no good unless you give a lot of money and show up at services five times a week."

"You know what? We're not pushing religion." Riley motioned toward Jillian. "This is my friend Jillian. I'm Riley." He stuck his hand out to the kid, and the boy returned a limp shake. "What's yours?"

"Mike." The kid stuffed his hands in the pockets of his hoodie and brought his foot down from the tree.

"Okay, Mike. I wanted to tell you about what happened to me."

The kid folded his arms over his chest and shrugged. "Why should I care?"

Riley tried to make eye-contact, but the boy wouldn't look at him. "Because, man, I don't want to see what happened to me happen to you."

Mike folded his arms over his chest. "What are you talking about?"

This wasn't as easy as he'd hoped. Riley tried to

clear his throat. "I used to come to this park to buy drugs. And to sell them to teens like you."

The boy lifted his chin and looked up at Riley with wide eyes.

He had the kid's attention now.

"You mean...you can sell me come coke?"

"No, buddy. I'm telling you I used to live that lifestyle, and I paid for it." Riley exhaled a long breath. "I got out of prison six months ago. I wasted ten years. My dream of being an accountant went down the toilet." Riley surprised himself with the rise in his tone. "I could've graduated by now and had a family." *And maybe a wife like Jillian.*

Jillian shifted her Bible from hand to hand and glanced from the boy to him.

"Hey, man." Mike stuffed his hands in the pockets of his jeans. "You were stupid and got caught. That's all."

Riley tightened his jaw. "Look. I don't know how many dealers *don't* get busted, but I sure saw a lot of them who did. I suspect the odds of a person not getting caught are way less than those who get arrested. But you're right, everyone gets stupid and taking drugs is really stupid."

"Lots of people use drugs, man. Only the dumb ones can't control it." The look in the teen's eyes told Riley the boy didn't believe his own words.

"You say that now, but when you spend time in prison, you'll have plenty of time to repeat over and over that you won't get caught." Riley wiped the sweat off his brow.

Mike gave him a sneer. "The first time people get busted, they don't go to jail. The state just gives you a talk and lets you go."

"Yeah, but it will still be on your record, and what about the next time? And the next? You probably think adults don't know anything, but I look back on my life. It sure would've been smarter to go to school, you know, man, to get a good job." His hand curled into a fist. "I don't have any rights, Mike. I can't carry a gun. I couldn't be a lawyer or teacher if I wanted to. Hey bud, I can't even travel to a lot of countries. I'm lucky Washington state lets me register to vote."

The boy looked at Riley and blew out a breath of air through puckered lips. "I guess you know what you're talking about."

"You can say that again. Look, your pal took off. I wish I'd had a chance to talk to him, but maybe you'll listen. When I asked God into my life in prison, I got a whole new attitude. In fact, I was like a new person. Jillian and I want to invite you to come to a youth meeting at our church next Sunday."

Mike sank back against the tree trunk again. "I don't have wheels, man."

"That's okay." Riley grinned. "There's going to be a bus here every Sunday at ten. It'll have Evergreen Fellowship on the side. We'll give you a ride, a meal, and a ride back. And you aren't going to some boring church service. We have a youth pastor who understands what teens are going through. Come on, Mike. If you don't like it, then don't come back next week. But every time you come, you'll get a good lunch, and I've never seen a teen turn down pizza and soda."

A tentative smile touched the kid's face. "Will you be there?"

"Yeah, me and Jillian. We help most Sundays." Riley held out his fist for a knuckle tap, and the kid bumped his fingers back. "Thanks, guy. I think I'll show up for a free meal. This once."

Mike gave them what Riley figured was a halfhearted smile. The kid sauntered off toward the falls.

"I have hopes for the boy." Riley knocked some more moisture off his brow and grinned at Jillian. "We've gotta keep praying for him."

Jillian giggled. "I was praying the whole time you were talking."

Riley ducked his head and focused on his shoes. "Yeah, guess I was a loud mouth." He looked up at Jillian with a smile. Something over her shoulder, toward the commons, caught his attention.

On the other side of the paved area, two teens stood side by side. Nothing unusual about that. Except the man hanging with them, with his hands stuffed in his pockets. Riley's radar went on high alert.

He squinted. Something familiar about him. *Hmm.* He had seen him somewhere before. An ominous cloud of uncertainty descended upon him. The guy looked like his old cellmate, James Pierce, but from this distance Riley couldn't be sure.

He was probably dealing drugs. Leading those foolish kids down the path of destruction. A muscle in Riley's jaw twitched. That was him ten years ago.

~

Jillian studied Riley's electric-blue eyes. They twinkled and his face held a glow that she could only guess reflected the peace God put in his life.

His eyes seemed to focus on something in the direction of the commons. A crease wrinkled his brow. What was he thinking about so hard? But then he shook his head, as if his concerns vanished.

Warmth traveled down her chest. Riley had spoken with confidence to the boy. After all, he'd lived the life. Who could be better equipped to minister to these kids? He was a testimony of the power of God to change a person's life. In many ways, she respected him more than she did than some of the doctors at the hospital.

True to his gentlemanly behavior, Riley held the door for her again and got into the driver's seat.

She studied him as he trained his attention on the afternoon downtown traffic. "I enjoyed working with you today. I learned about ministering to teens from watching you."

Riley glanced her way and to the road again. "Thanks, Jillian." A rosy flush filled his cheeks.

She laughed. "I don't know many men who could talk to kids like that. You deserve a lot of credit. I still feel bad about the night Dr. Camp shoved you. You showed a lot more grace than he did."

"I never expected you to say that. Actually, I wasn't sure you'd speak to me again after I told you about my prison record."

"I think that's the best part about having a Christian friend. We're not going to criticize each other." The memories of yesterday, the secrets they'd revealed to each other, nagged her—not Riley's but hers. She slipped a tube of gloss from her purse and applied it to her dry lips. Should she have exposed her past to him? But he'd comforted her without judging her. She could still feel his arms around her while she cried.

Contentment permeated her body. Riley wasn't afraid to divulge his past, either. Her Christian brother trusted her with all the details of his incarceration too. He'd held nothing back.

Chapter Ten

As long as Jillian practiced medicine, she'd never cease to be amazed at the miracle of childbirth. She floated out of Room 214 and into the hospital hall. Another life had come into the world.

Her patient couldn't have had an easier time. She was a veteran—her fourth. When Jillian had placed the red, squalling baby boy on Mom's chest, the joy on her face was worth all the hard work it had taken to become a doctor.

She pulled off her latex gloves and peered down the hall. Sunshine streamed in from the windows, bathing the walls and floor in golden warmth. Farther down, she could see the door to the hospital gardens. A little air and a moment alone might do her some good before the clinic claimed her for the rest of the day.

With her first step through the door, the pungent aroma of the fragrant Douglas Firs enveloped her. Jillian breathed deep, trying to take in enough of the heady scent to store in her memory all afternoon. Rays of sunlight glinted off the leaves of the elm tree and rhododendron bushes. The cedar bench under a Douglas fir invited her to sit.

Jett had hinted the night at the Space Needle that he

intended to give her a diamond. She leaned back and relaxed, running her hand over her left ring finger. Marriage, to Jett. She still hadn't formed a definite conclusion what she'd say to a proposal, though she leaned toward saying yes.

From her peripheral vision, she sensed motion to her left.

Farther down the lane that ran through the gardens, Jett leaned against a plum tree, his arms folded on his chest.

She smiled. Guess he had the same idea—a quick visit to the great outdoors. She rose from her seat and wandered along the concrete-paved path.

He must've heard her footsteps, as he turned toward her with a smile. "I was thinking about you. To be honest—about us."

Jett's broad shoulders, clean-shaven handsome face, and tall frame attracted her. "Me, too."

When he arrived at her side, he curled his fingers around her hand and lifted it to his lips. "I've got the perfect ring picked out. I'm pretty sure you'll like it."

Hmm. He's wearing his doctor persona. As if letting the patient know who's in charge. She'd witnessed his authoritative, commanding nature many times before, the same front he conveyed today.

"It must be beautiful." Could she really doubt his sincerity? He wouldn't go to the trouble of paying so much attention to her if he didn't care. Besides, he wasn't dating anyone else.

"You're worth it, Jillian. I couldn't ask for a better wife. You're pretty, smart, and you understand the demands of my career." He threw his head back and raised his chin. "The chief of staff at Woodlyn would be mighty impressed if I married another doctor. Especially one of your quality."

My quality? Was she a stepping-stone in his climb to the top? What about love? "Jett, I understand your ambition. But you need to understand mine as well."

"You mean that free clinic you mention so often? Jillian, honestly, how do you expect to get ahead if that's your goal?" He pulled her into his arms and whispered, his lips near her ear. "Hey, Babe. This is a phase you're going through. Once you're married to me, you'll forget all about it. You'll have something more interesting to think about—me." His woodland scent enveloped her as his lips smoothed over her cheek, then nibbled at her ear.

With a gentle push on his chest, she whispered. "Not here, Jett."

She ignored the uneasy feeling in her stomach. The gardens weren't appropriate for kissing. Someone could be looking out of the many windows. Surely, that's what caused this new sensation.

~

A fifteen-minute break from cleaning hospital floors would do him some good. Riley nudged the door open into the hot summer sunshine. The path led to the wooden bench under the Douglas fir. This time of year brought back memories of summer vacation when he was a kid. Three whole months of freedom.

Yet those days were gone. He wasn't a teen anymore. He ran a hand over his mouth. Only one week left of the day shift before summer classes began. He sank down on the seat and filled his lungs with a long breath of the fresh air. Couldn't mess up this chance to prove he could be responsible—attend class, work his night job, and find time to hit the books.

The library at the community college offered a wealth of information on financial aid. The possibility of receiving funding from a private Christian organization looked positive. Thankfully, he'd be able to finance part of his classes himself. *Thank you, Jesus.*

Only a few more minutes, and he'd have to go in. Riley shut his eyes and allowed the healing rays of the sun to warm him. He rubbed the stiffness out of his neck and exhaled. When he opened his eyes, he allowed his focus to move around the perimeter of the gardens.

Jillian stood with her back to him in Dr. Camp's embrace. The arrogant doctor kissed her cheek.

Riley's blood ran hot. His first instinct was to yank her out of the obnoxious Dr. Camp's arms and punch him. Bet he wouldn't be kissing anyone with his lips busted.

Common sensed returned. Why should he care if they embraced? What concern was it of his? Heart pounding, he jumped to his feet and tramped to the door. He needed to get away.

Why did he seethe when he saw the hug? Ten years ago, he'd exploited Jillian and bragged to his friends about his conquest. Now, everything had changed. Riley shook his head, swung the door open, and stepped into the hall. Jillian was a Christian sister whom he respected and... No, he couldn't admit it, but the truth emerged. Dr. Jett Camp held in his arms the woman Riley had fallen for.

Chapter Eleven

The typical Sunday afternoon strollers, picnickers, and joggers filled the park's main section. The boy at the edge of the commons hadn't taken his eyes off Riley from the minute he began his story. The teen's designer jeans, expensive tennis shoes, and intelligent conversation amazed Jillian.

When she first envisioned young people who purchased drugs, she hadn't stopped to think that some might come from affluent homes. The guy appeared to be wrapped up in every word Riley said, like the two had really connected.

Surely the kid couldn't deny the validity in Riley's words. He'd lived the nightmare, paid for his crimes, and come through it a better man.

Jillian caught her breath when she trained her gaze on Riley and the teen again. Riley had his hand on the boy's shoulder. They both bowed their heads.

"And I ask You Lord to honor Jayke's confession of faith. In Jesus name. Amen." Riley lifted his head and gave the guy's shoulder a couple of pats. "Angels are rejoicing, man. They always do when a person gives their life to God."

Jayke raised his face to Riley and blinked. He

curved away from them and batted at a tear on his cheek. When he turned back, his face flushed, like a student who'd just received a scholarship for college. "I'll be on that bus Sunday, man. If God could change you like that, I know he could help me. I...I want to hear more."

"Okay, buddy." Riley slapped the kid's shoulder. "You'll never regret asking Jesus into your life. I'm nobody special. He'll do the same for you and make all the difference."

Jayke gave Riley a high-five and stuffed his hands in his pockets as he ambled toward the sidewalk. He peered off to where the other two teens loitered. They laughed, making a raucous noise filled with shoulder punches and heavy-handed shoving. Jayke watched a moment longer, shrugged, and turned toward the street.

"Praise the Lord, Jillian." Riley pulled his elbow down in a victory sign. "I think we made a real difference in that boy's life."

"Only God could've lit up your face with such joy. Your eyes shone like you'd seen a glimpse of Heaven." Her ministry partner was the sweetest guy she knew. He'd come a long way from a drug dealer to a man who gave teens the good news about God. *Awesome.*

Riley's cheeks turned pink, and he stared at the grass. "Cool."

"I never dreamed we could reach a boy like that." She fought the wayward tear attempting to escape. "He probably has everything the world offers—money, a comfortable lifestyle. Riley, I..." How could she tell him how important this ministry was to her. How important he'd become in her heart, the two of them doing God's work in Cascade Waterfall Park? "I'm not giving you much help, but I'm still learning a lot."

He studied his tennis shoes for a moment, then looked at her. "Hey, don't forget how Jamie showed up at the teen meeting this morning and opened up. Thanks to you."

An errant strand of hair fell to his forehead. She resisted the urge to brush it back. His penetrating gaze, his lips parted in a grin, caused a flutter she hadn't expected.

"I really think we made a difference with her as well. She told me she's considering putting her baby up for adoption. Thank God she didn't abort it like she'd planned."

He lifted his focus toward the commons.

The sound of live classical music floated through the air. "The Sunday Concert Under the Stars." She shot him a grin. "That's probably not your kind of music."

"I'm a Country Western fan," Riley scratched his head, "but I'll give it a try. Might be fun."

Circular stepping-stones led through a grove of poplar and elms to a gazebo with a raised wooden platform. A garden of summer blooms and ferns surrounded the base of the structure.

A group of four musicians played the classical guitar, the flute, a cello, and a viola. People sat around on the grass in clusters, some on blankets and others in lawn chairs.

Riley ran a hand through his hair. "To be honest, I'm not up on classical music. What's that they're playing?"

"It's a Beethoven concerto." She gazed in the direction of the soothing tones. "I've got it on a CD in my car."

They plopped down on the grass behind a couple more interested in each other than the music. Jillian hugged her knees to her chest and let the melody fill her soul. "Beethoven had an amazing story. God must've been at work in his life. The man composed music despite being deaf."

"Wow. If I wrote a song, it would probably sound like my old dog Spot howling at the moon." Riley winked at her, leaned back on his elbows, and crossed his ankles.

"You're too funny." Jillian laughed. The airy poetic notes of the flute blended with the quiet chords of the guitar. Delight surged in her. The music swelled with the passion the composer must've wanted to convey.

Riley pushed up to a seated position and looked from the musicians to her. "How could Beethoven create music if he was deaf?"

"He heard it in his head." Jillian rested her chin on her knees. The rich sounds softened into a whisper as the musicians rose to their feet and placed their instruments on their chairs. The crowd clapped and whistled when the performers bent from their waists in unison.

From the corner of her eye, she sensed Riley looking at her as if trying to find an answer to a question. When she turned his way, he averted his eyes, probably embarrassed she'd found him staring.

As the crowd began folding their chairs and blankets, Riley offered his hand and helped her up. "I enjoyed that. I think I can appreciate classical music a little more. But I'll have to admit, your company made it more interesting."

Jillian's face warmed, and she answered in a quiet

voice. "I like being with you, too." She couldn't tell him how relaxed she felt in his presence. Or how fond she'd become of him.

They threaded their way through the crowd of music lovers, some still lazing about on the grass and chatting with others. When they stepped into the crosswalk of the busy downtown street, Riley's warm, firm hand grasped hers. No way could she ignore the feel of his skin next to hers and how her hand felt secure within his masculine grip.

What's my problem? Riley's only acting like a gentleman while we cross the street.

When they arrived at the sidewalk and headed down the block to Riley's car, he hadn't released her hand as she'd expected, though she didn't mind.

Finally when they reached his car, he stopped and scratched his neck, giving her the same questioning look. He paused, moving closer to her with parted lips. *Is he going to kiss me?*

He shook his head as if waking up from a dream, squeezed her fingers, and released them. With a hand on the passenger door, he opened it, and she slid in.

A twinge of guilt coursed through her. Should she be holding hands with him? She and Jett were almost engaged, though she didn't have the ring yet.

Riley lowered into the driver's seat and started the ignition.

She enjoyed the feel of his touch, but she could explain it. He was an amazing Christian friend. *Of course. That was the reason. Right?*

~

Riley pulled up next to Jillian's late model Lexus parked in the church lot and rushed out of his car. By the time he reached the passenger door, Jillian had already stepped out and clicked the remote, unlocking her car.

If he had his choice, he'd spend the rest of the evening with her. Yet, he needed to deny his new feelings. She probably saw him as a ministry partner and nothing more. He couldn't expect a doctor like Jillian to find an interest in someone who scrubbed the floors where she worked. "Bye. Until next Sunday or at the hospital." He tried to keep his tone casual and hoped he'd see her sooner rather than later.

As if in no hurry to leave, Jillian leaned against her car door. Her pink lips parted. Was she granting him permission to kiss her?

Riley fought what he wanted to do most, explore the moist skin of her mouth, like he almost did after the concert.

For a second he considered drawing her into his arms and confessing the truth, telling her how sorry he was for their past. He reached to brush a stand of hair from her face but got control of himself and jerked his hand to his side. *No, I can't. Not now.*

This woman meant more to him than ever, and he despised what he'd done to her, what he put her through. He turned from her trusting aquamarine eyes. "Thank you for today, Jillian. For your prayers…for being my ministry partner. I…" He had to walk away before he started stuttering like an idiot. "Good night."

He dragged his feet on the pavement and traipsed around the front of his car. After he slid into the driver's seat, he glanced in his rearview mirror.

With a smile, she waved as she backed out.

When her Lexus disappeared around the corner, Riley tapped his fist on the dashboard of his Chevy. He shouldn't have held her hand. What if she got the wrong idea? Yet she hadn't pulled away. He couldn't imagine why not. Surely she wasn't attracted to an ex-con. Especially not with that suave, prosperous doctor chasing her.

For the umpteenth time, Riley chided himself. He didn't stand a chance with her. And even if the unheard of happened, once she learned the truth—that he was the father of her baby, the one who'd caused her pain and heartache, she'd flee from him.

Jillian, the sweet Christian woman he'd fallen for. Riley dropped his face into his hands. An image of the young innocent girl formed in his mind. That night ten years ago, she'd had way too much beer which made it worse.

He clutched two handfuls of hair and squeezed hard. In his mind's eye, the younger Jillian squirmed in the waiting room chair at the women's health clinic. She faced the benign smile of the administrator who said they would take care of her. Only a matter of removing the unwanted tissue. Later, she lay on a hard, surgical table, and left the clinic minus the life that had begun to form and grow inside her.

Alone. She probably endured the procedure with no one by her side. Not even the father of her baby.

What Jillian suffered was far worse than anything he had experienced in prison, even the time another inmate held a knife to his throat, and he thought his life was over. Guilt ate at his gut. She'd told him the whole truth, but he was too much of a coward to be honest with her. How much lower could he sink?

He didn't deserve her, the brave and godly woman he loved with all his heart. He covered his face with both hands. A sob erupted from his throat. Then another. And another. Riley couldn't stop the tears or the moans.

Chapter Twelve

Riley emptied the last trashcan into the receptacle on the cart and examined the waiting room of Dr. Murphy's dental office. He'd vacuumed the carpet, cleaned and restocked the restrooms, and dusted the counters.

Dexter would approve of his finishing touches, placing the scattered magazines back in the wall racks. His boss had sacrificed for him, creating this job and keeping him on even after he messed up. Dex had been right about Riley's history of taking shortcuts. But no more.

He glanced at his watch. Nine. He'd have a few hours to hit the books tonight before he turned in. No shortcuts with school either. If he could earn a degree, he could prove to Mom he was no longer the wild, fraternity boy-turned-criminal.

One more thing before he left. He pushed the cart back into the janitor's closet and locked the door with his master key. The long hall ahead led to the back door of the building.

"Beautiful Things" sounded from his pocket. *Hmm.* Jillian. He needed to ignore the way his heart skipped a beat. "Hello, Dr. Coleman."

"Riley. Riley." Her voice sounded strained and hoarse.

The muscle in his jaw twitched. "Jillian, what's wrong?"

"Get to the hospital, please, as soon as you can. I need you."

"Are you okay?"

"Yes. Please come to the labor and delivery ward."

"I'm on my way."

He barely remembered the drive or his trip up the elevator to the second floor. Jillian said she was okay. Then what could possibly be wrong? Maybe her boyfriend was ill. Riley gave himself a mental kick. She wouldn't call him for that.

His stomach rolled, sending bile to his throat. He knew why she called. *She's found me out.* A shudder took him. Perspiration rolled down his neck.

The elevator doors opened. Riley stepped out and looked up and down the hall. No Jillian. He walked to the nurse's station a few steps to his left.

A nurse whose nametag read Mrs. Duncan, RN, glanced up at him. "Yes, sir."

"I'm Riley Mathis. I…uh…received a call from Dr. Coleman. She asked me to meet her here." Even a deep breath didn't still his pounding pulse.

Mrs. Duncan's face grew solemn, and her smile disappeared. "Yes, Riley Mathis. She's in emergency surgery. She asked if you could wait for her. The lounge is two doors down the hall."

He knew where to find the waiting room. He'd cleaned every inch of the floor. "Sure. I'll be in there when she comes out." Riley sidled down the hall and dropped onto the leather couch in the empty room. He rested his elbows on his knees with his face in his hands.

Icy fingers gripped his spine. How had Jillian discovered his identity? Maybe she suddenly remembered him from a gesture or facial expression. Or perhaps she'd talked with an old college friend who'd seen them stumbling up the stairs at the frat house.

Riley gripped the edge of the couch. He had to tell her. The time had come. He cared about Jillian more than he wanted to admit. They'd become friends, but now the truth threatened to unhinge him. Making matters worse, he loved her more than himself. His life would never be the same without her by his side. But how could she ever forgive him? He'd ruined her life.

His heart sank lower than ever before. Lower than when the board denied parole the first time.

Tonight would be the last time he'd ever see Jillian Coleman. He'd bet his college tuition on the grim fact that stared at him from the shrinking walls of the waiting room.

"I can do all things through Christ who strengthens me. I can do all things through Christ who strengthens me." He put his head in his hands again and closed his eyes. "Give me the words when I see her, dear Lord. Give me the courage to act like a man and confess my sin to Jillian. Make something beautiful out of the dust of my mistake...and hers."

The cushioned couch pillow brought no comfort when he rested his head back and closed his eyes. He'd never hold her hand again or go to another concert under the stars with her. A vice squeezed his gut. He'd lose his ministry partner and would never hold her in his arms again.

After a while, he opened his eyes. He'd been there an hour, according to the clock on the wall. He'd have to initiate the confession the minute she returned from surgery.

"Riley." Jillian stood in the doorway, her surgical cap in her hand. Her white mask hung around her neck and dangled on her chest. Dark circles marred her eyes. She ran a hand over her brow.

He bolted up and took a few steps toward her, planted his feet to the floor, and willed his pulse to slow.

She remained frozen to the spot and stared at him a long moment.

A silent Jillian. Maybe shocked and angry. He didn't blame her.

She opened her mouth.

"Wait, before you say anything. I was..."

Jillian rushed to him and fell against his chest, throwing her arms around his shoulders.

Though her nearness thrilled him, he didn't understand her actions. He held her and ran his hand over her hair as she cried. "Shh, Jillian. Whatever it is, we'll face it together."

Savoring the feel of her body so close to his, Riley closed his eyes. When he opened them, a glaring Dr. Camp stood at the door, his lips pressed together in a tight line. Then he lifted his chin and stomped off down the hall. If the doctor cared so much about Jillian, why wouldn't he want to comfort her?

Finally her sobs subsided, and she slid from his embrace, lifting red eyes to him. "Thank you for coming."

Thank you? She was thanking him? His mind

whirled in a thousand directions. Maybe he'd been mistaken about her finding him out. "Anytime you're hurt...I want to be there for you, to comfort you." He'd better stuff a gag down his throat before he told her how he felt about her. "But I don't understand. What's wrong?"

"I came from surgery just now." Jillian's voice dropped to a whisper. "A young girl had a medical abortion a couple of days ago." She shivered.

Riley took her hand and led her to the couch, edging down beside her.

"The chemicals didn't do the job." She covered her face with her hands. "There was a problem."

Though the issue appeared to be serious, would Jillian, as a physician, become so emotionally distraught over a patient? Was that why she called him to the hospital, to pray for the procedure? "The baby?"

"The substances killed the baby, but the abortion was incomplete." Jillian's lips trembled as she nodded. "She suffered with excessive hemorrhaging and developed a pelvic infection." Jillian tightened her grip on his hand. "She was afraid to seek treatment until now, afraid her parents would find out."

"The girl? How is she?"

"She's stable." Jillian's eyes pleaded with him. He wanted to help her, but he couldn't if he didn't know what she expected of him. *God, help me.*

"She's only eighteen." Jillian grasped both his hands in hers and held them tight. "Her dad's an attorney."

He didn't have to ask any more questions. Against all hope, he prayed he was wrong. "Jamie," he whispered. Yet any illusion of optimism crumbled.

"Yes. She granted me permission to tell you. You

were there for her from the start." Jillian squeezed her eyes shut and whispered. "I never thought she'd do it. She'd promised…"

He lifted his hand to comfort her, but nothing he'd say would help. They were so sure Jamie had worked things out, that she chose not to go through with it.

Now another innocent life was lost. A stab of guilt and regret wrenched through Riley's gut. Jamie's decision slashed his heart to shreds.

His and Jillian's baby had been ripped from her ten years ago, like Jamie's. If he hadn't clung to Jillian, they might've both slipped to the floor.

Then it hit him. No one had held her the day she aborted their child. She'd borne the pain alone. The consequences of his recklessness smacked him like a fist to his face.

Somewhere there was another kid, the other half of a shallow relationship with Jamie. His carelessness had caused the death of a child who deserved to live. Riley tightened his jaw.

"I'm sorry." Riley cuddled her and glided one hand along her shoulder and the other across her back. "I'm so sorry, Jillian." He was no better than the kid who got Jamie pregnant. He regretted Jamie's loss. But his words spoke of more than the teen's failure. His heart ached for another child who'd died. His child.

"She just wouldn't wait for help, Riley." Jillian didn't let go. She slipped her arms around his neck, and her tears dampened his shirt. Her shoulders shook again. "She made the same mistake…"

The heat of remorse swept over him, and he couldn't restrain the tears that fell from his eyes, blending with hers.

When Jillian finally pulled away, a lump formed in Riley's throat threatening to strangle him. He'd planned to tell her the secret he'd held from her. But now how could he place that stress on her when she suffered the pain of Jamie's loss?

Chapter Thirteen

"Everything looks great." Jillian caught Holly's arm and helped her sit up on the exam table. "Your baby is developing right on schedule. I bet Timmy will be excited to have a little sister."

Holly rested her hand on her belly. "He can't wait to be a big brother."

"I'm envious of you and Jess." Jillian looked at the wall chart with the stages of fetal development. "You two did it the right way." An all too familiar wave of regret washed over her. She lowered her eyes. Would the guilt ever go away? "As I've shared with you, I made some pretty bad choices in college. I keep wishing I could make up for the past." She handed Holly her prosthesis.

"Sweetie, we all make mistakes." Holly squeezed Jillian's hand. "As you know, I lost a baby when I was in college because of my own foolishness." Holly attached the prosthesis under her knee. "The same night I lost my leg."

Jillian supported Holly's elbow as she placed her right foot on the floor until she could stand without support.

"You know the story. That day on the back of my

boyfriend's motorcycle, I thought I was invincible, until the accident. I didn't tell him until years later that I had miscarried our child that night."

Lightening flamed through Jillian's stomach. At least Holly hadn't aborted her baby. *What I did was much worse.* "But look at your life now. God has given you a wonderful Christian husband and another chance at motherhood." Jillian's shoulders sagged. Guilt, her constant companion for years, left her drained.

Holly had lost so much, but she refused to let it defeat her. She'd lived through her problems to be the strong, self-confident woman standing here today. How did she keep from wallowing in remorse? Jillian admired her tenacity. What she wouldn't give to have it, too.

"I love the second chapter of Joel where it describes how God restores to us the years the locust have eaten." Holly flashed her an understanding smile. "He's blessed me with an amazing family. God is faithful."

Jillian appreciated the scripture in principle, but to let the words seep into her soul and allow the truth to manifest in her life—not an easy task. The place in her heart her baby had occupied felt like an empty cavern filled with echoes of the past. Would God ever permit her to have a husband and another child?

Jett wants to be my husband, but I have so many doubts. Does he love me for me, or am I a boost to his career?

With a shake of her head, she drew her thoughts to her patient. "Holly. You're all set until your next appointment. Don't forget the prenatal vitamins." Jillian patted her patient's shoulder and opened the exam room door.

Lord, Your word was true for Holly—making up for what she lost. But I don't think it's possible for me. My mistake was too grave.

Jillian slunk into her office and closed the door. If she stayed busy, maybe she wouldn't have to think of her past and the heaviness in her heart. She picked up Holly's file and jotted down the entries for today's appointment. But that earlier time in her life, her irrevocable mistake filled her mind again. *Who am I kidding?*

One minute to clear her head. She shut her eyes and leaned back in her leather chair. The young fraternity man had coaxed her upstairs. She knew what he wanted. All her friends were doing it. Dizziness had overwhelmed her in the darkened room. She couldn't recall anything about him except he'd held her in a way she'd never experienced before.

He'd surprised her with his gentle kisses, not at all demanding, as she might have expected. He'd whispered words that comforted her, though she couldn't remember now what he said. The guy had showed her attention and acceptance.

A mental image of her workaholic father usurped the picture of the young man. She could visualize the stern expression he usually wore. How he'd return from his committee meetings at church only to point out the one math problem she'd gotten wrong on the homework she'd worked on for two hours. After all, electrical engineers were sticklers for detail.

But what else could she have done to please him all those years? She tried so hard to garner his praise. Even went to medical school when he suggested it, though she wanted it, too. Dad loved her, but he didn't accept her unconditionally like Mom.

Like changing channels on a TV, the college man and that night flashed back into her mind. Though she'd been raving drunk, she still had to admit the truth. She'd allowed his actions. And they filled a longing within her.

Sitting up straight in her chair, her eyes flew open. She didn't even know his name. Did he still live in Washington? What would he say if he knew he'd fathered a child?

Jillian rubbed her forehead and forced her attention to the appointment calendar. She read the name. Roxanne Garrett.

With her patient's chart in her hand, she headed toward the second exam room on the other side of her office. The nurse would have Roxanne ready by now.

She tapped on the closed door.

"Yes, come in," the muffled voice answered.

Pushing a smile in place, she stepped into the room.

Dangling her legs off the edge of the exam table, her patient waited, her hospital gown wrapped around her.

"How's the new mama?" She glanced down at her notation from Roxanne's last appointment.

Tim's wife smoothed her hand over her large belly. "It's getting harder to stand all day at my salon, but I can't exactly work on people's hair sitting down. I'm trying not to schedule appointments too close together."

"Uh, oh. I need to book an appointment for highlights in a couple of weeks." Jillian laughed and helped Roxy lie back on the exam table. "Who's going to oversee your shop while you're out?"

"I've got several girls working for me now,

including Mandy Jones who used to be in Tim's old youth group from Woodlyn Fellowship." Roxanne scooted up a bit higher on the table. "Tim's sister Janelle is going to oversee the day-to-day operation while I'm out with the baby. My mom's keeping the books."

"So you're planning to go back to work?" Jillian peered down at the perky young woman.

"Yes. I've invested too much time and money in the shop to give it up. The baby will come with me." She giggled. "If Tim's off, he can babysit."

"You know, Roxie, your husband is a blessing in the mission's ministry. He has such a heart for teens." Jillian moved her hands over Roxanne's belly to check the size of her uterus.

"He does, though things were pretty tough for him at Woodlyn Fellowship." She cleared her throat. "He helped me understand how to be obedient to the Lord." She folded fingers over her chest. "He showed me a better way."

Moving the stethoscope around on Roxy's stomach, Jillian listened to the steady beat of the baby's heart. "At least you didn't make my mistake. Not a day goes by that I don't think of it." *Here I go again. Leaning on one of my patients.* She clasped her mouth shut, but it was too late. Oh, well. Holly and Roxanne were her sisters in the Lord, and her friends.

"I'm sorry, Jillian. But you know, if someone commits the sin in her heart or mind, it's the same thing in God's eyes. Once before I gave my life to the Lord, I thought I was pregnant. I had decided to abort the baby. I found out later I wasn't, but I still committed the sin. So you see, you're not the only person in the world to make that mistake." Roxanne's gentle rub on Jillian's hand soothed her like a warm cup of cocoa on a frigid day. "God has forgiven you for what happened. I know because Tim assures me daily that the Lord no longer remembers *my* sinful past—or his."

That's fine for them, but I can't get to that place of assurance no matter how hard I try. "Pray for me when you think about it."

"You've got it." Roxy's large blue eyes locked with Jillian's. "What about the father? How did the situation impact him?"

"It was long ago...I was wasted." Warmth spread on Jillian's face. "I don't know who he is, but I'm sure he has no idea he fathered a child."

"Well, we might not know who he is, but God does. I'll pray for him as well."

"I suppose I need to pray for him, too." The tension in Jillian's neck eased. "Hey, lady. The baby's heartbeat is strong and everything looks fine. All you have to do is make sure you don't work too hard, and let Tim pamper you."

Jillian gave her a wave as she left. "See you at your next appointment." She shut the door so Roxanne could get dressed.

The view from her office window looked out over the green expanse behind the building. Holly and Roxanne chose life for their babies. Yes, Roxanne *thought* about having an abortion, but no way were the long-term consequences the same. She didn't have to live with this constant misery.

Jillian's shoulders tightened up again. If only Jamie had made that choice.

The image of the frightened teenager lying in bed

filled her memory. Would Jamie suffer as she had? Would she regret what she'd done?

Only God's love could reach her now. Only He could give her hope. The Lord longed for Jamie to turn to Him, cry out to Him, and let Him take all this pain and sorrow away. Then she could move forward.

God, help me to be an extension of Your arms in this teenager's life.

Chapter Fourteen

Riley dropped his blue vinyl backpack on the worn sofa and wandered into the kitchen. His parched tongue demanded water. In the door of the fridge, several bottles of the clear, chilled liquid waited. He twisted the cap, took a long swig, and plopped down on the couch.

His Financial Accounting textbook rested on top of the spiral notebooks in his backpack. Hard to believe. Riley Mathis, a college student again. His chest expanded with a deep breath as his fingers slid over the slick cover of the book. In this class alone he'd learn how to make better decisions in personal and organizational finances.

One day maybe he'd be able to offer advice to Dexter, if his stepfather would accept it, and make wise decisions with his own budget.

All the money he'd wasted on drugs in the past was enough to make his head throb. Selling them to get rich made it worse. *Downright stupid.*

Prison had knocked some sense into him, but the day he turned his life over to the Lord began the slow process for the change he'd experienced in his thinking. With every Bible verse he read, God impressed on him truths from scripture. Thank the Lord He was patient. Now Riley respected the principle that income came honestly through hard work and smart choices.

The road ahead might not be easy. He crossed an ankle over his knee. But one thing he'd become convinced of: his Lord was an expert in making something beautiful out of the chaos humans brought on themselves.

A yellow highlighter poked out from the side pocket of his backpack. A goal of two chapters every night sounded reasonable. He flipped open the text to chapter one.

Tap, tap. Seemed odd someone would knock. Most people rang the bell. He clambered to his feet and unbolted the door. Probably an over-zealous cult member inviting him to church.

Riley gaped at the man standing on his threshold. James Pierce? What was his cellmate from prison doing here after all this time? The long, unkempt hair and two-day-old beard James sported struck a familiar chord. He'd seen him more recently at the park dealing drugs.

"Hey, Riley, old pal." James cocked an eyebrow and smirked. "Long time no see."

"What do you want?" Riley stepped out on the porch. "How did you know where I live?"

"Simple. I saw my old buddy in the park the other day with a chick. You two were chatting with a couple of customers. When you took off, I followed you. I didn't want to interrupt anything you had going with the babe. But you surprised me and stopped by some church. The hot mama got out of your car, then you drove here."

The man standing on Riley's porch in slacks and sports shirt was a complete contrast to the felon Riley had last seen in handcuffs and an orange jumpsuit. "Look, man. I'm not sure why you're here, but I'm pretty busy right now. I'm studying for a class."

James swiveled his head from side to side peering up and down the street. "Look, dude. Can I come in? I just want to talk for a minute."

Riley hesitated, then stepped back to allow the cocky man in.

His cellmate scrutinized the room before taking possession of Riley's lone easy chair. "So this is where you live? Kind of a dump, if you ask me. You could do a lot better."

The muscles in Riley's jaws tensed. Tim Garrett's former home was a godsend. He couldn't have asked for a better deal from the owner, Jess Colton. Far better than a small jail cell.

He grasped his accounting book and moved it on the coffee table then sat down on the couch. "I'm happy here. It's big enough for me." He caught his upper lip between his teeth. "A friend from church rents it to me."

"Church? You're still into those fairytales? I figured once you got your freedom, you wouldn't mess around with religion anymore. Face it, man. You needed a crutch while you were behind bars. But you're free now. Live a little."

James's misguided prattle assaulted Riley's composure. If James considered Jesus' forgiveness a crutch, then he'd admit to needing one. Life since that day the guy from Prison Fellowship led him in prayer held more purpose than ever before. Being a Christian brought him joy and peace, something his old life never did.

"What do you want here?" The dealer's presence in Riley's home disgusted him. His neck flushed hot. James could only be up to no good, probably trying to draw him back into old habits.

"Don't you remember?" James tilted his head to one side and sneered. "We used to be buddies." Sarcasm sheathed each word and transformed them into ominous darts. "Remember all those nights when we'd lie in our bunks after they turned the lights off? We'd talk about how things would be when we got out. How we could start up a business, add more dealers and expand?" He leaned closer to Riley and held out two open palms. "Do you want to live in this dump forever?"

"Hey, I'm grateful to have this place. And no, I'm not going to live here forever. I'm in college now and hope to become an accountant."

"How long does that take?"

"What do you care?" Riley couldn't control the tight timbre of his voice. "I'll be done in less than four years if I work hard at it."

James threw his head back and let go with a raucous laugh. "Four years? You're crazy, man. If you joined up with me like we talked about, I could have you out of this place in a couple of months. You'd be living the good life."

Help James sell drugs? Was he crazy? They'd spent ten years in jail already. Did he want to try a double-or-nothing?

Riley sucked in a deep breath and expelled slowly, but that didn't ease the knot in his gut. James didn't have a conscience. Never considered the ramifications of selling narcotics to teens beyond how it lined his pockets and gave him his own fogged high. Men did all kinds of crazy things while under the influence including using innocent girls. Riley winced at the thought. If anyone knew from experience, he did.

The image of Jamie came unbidden. Pain-wracked, bleeding. Some kid had gotten her pregnant. Was he high when he took advantage of her?

Regret and guilt careened through Riley's heart. He'd been no better. "Look. My life is different now. I'm not interested in dealing drugs anymore."

James puffed out his chest. "Hey, guy. You wouldn't be on your own. I have a few more contacts. If we all combine forces, sell to more of those stupid kids, become a bigger organization, our income could increase faster. Makes good business sense."

Riley tensed his shoulders. He was well acquainted with the destructive pattern James described. Once it had attracted him, but now he despised it. They'd give a kid a free sample. Then when the teen was hooked, they'd demand payment, increasing the price every time. He didn't use to care if the kid had to steal to feed his habit, as long as he got his money.

Thoughts of the past made him squirm. He didn't want to ruin people's lives any more but to help them find freedom in Christ.

Fury ballooned in his chest, forcing him to his feet. He yanked James up by the front of his shirt. Got right in his face. "I've already been down that road. It's a dead end. My life changed in prison. Permanently. No matter what you think, God is in my life now." Riley tightened the muscles in his arms and shoved James toward the front door. "Get out."

James gasped, his eyes as round as the plastic plates in the prison chow hall. He took a few stumbling steps toward the door.

"If I ever...*ever* see you in that park trying to sell those kids' lives down the toilet, I'll do everything I can to stop you, including going to the cops. I wasn't dealing to those kids. You couldn't have been more wrong. It's none of your business, but my friend and I were telling that boy about God. About how He can make a difference in his life."

Riley opened the front door, grasped James' shirt collar, and pushed him out.

With a few stumbling steps backward, James held up two palms. "Okay, okay. I get it. But I'm telling you, you're going to regret this someday. When you come crawling back to me begging me to bring you into the organization, I'll tell you where you can go." He turned around and stomped down the sidewalk. As he turned the corner, he lifted his finger in an obscene gesture.

A cold dose of reality settled over Riley. He had no control over James. Couldn't prevent him or others like him from doing their dirty work. "Merciful God, bring the gospel to the lives of the teens in this town. Please make James hungry for you. Change his life as You did mine."

The blind soul he used to be branded him. He covered his eyes and thought of the times he stood in the park and on street corners. He made as many sales as he could without the cops catching on. What a scum ball he'd been.

But not even his bitter tears could erase the past. Only God's grace could do that. Like Peter from the Bible who even denied he knew the Lord, he had received God's mercy.

Riley slammed the door, locked it, and rested his head against the cool surface. "Dear Lord, I'm grateful that You changed my life. Seeing James today only makes me want to work harder at the park."

He pushed away from the door and straightened. A strange notion hit him. He needed a dog.

JUNE FOSTER

Chapter Fifteen

Riley backed out of the parking lot of the metal prefab building, pleased with his decision. The memory of James's appearance made him feel dirty. But more than that, it reinforced his gut feeling that he needed to get a dog. His old cellmate knew where he lived now, and he'd be back. *An early warning system* for uninvited visitors at his small house had become a necessity now.

The sign Woodlyn Animal Shelter caught his attention as he pulled onto the street. *Whew*. The paperwork had seemed endless, but finally he completed all of it. Listing references seemed a bit much, like applying for a job or something. But since they required it, he'd complied. Hopefully Tim Garrett and Jess Colton would give him a good report.

Riley glanced in the rearview mirror at the pile of items in his backseat he'd acquired before he went to the pound. A water bowl, a few pet toys, and a variety of dog food and treats. His sweet Mom blessed him, always wanting to help in some way. When she gave him Spot's old fluffy blanket where their pet had slept before he died, he couldn't deny his gratitude that his mother was willing to donate it to him.

Now all he had to do was wait. The shelter said he'd hear something soon. Riley headed toward his house. He'd unload the stuff Mom gave him and figure out how he could make his house more pet friendly.

~

The bowl of potato salad rested on the front passenger's seat. Riley grabbed it, slid out, and closed the door with his foot. Back in high school, he'd been a pro at making the recipe when Mom let him loose in the kitchen. Now he wasn't so sure this dish held to his old standards.

The singles potluck and fellowship would do him some good, hanging out with other Christians. Besides, Jillian would be there. Maybe he'd ask her to go with him later to the pound, since they called this morning and said he'd been approved. One day's wait wasn't bad. He juggled the dish in one hand and waved at Pastor Taylor's son with bags of chips in their arms.

Riley walked through the double doors and to the fellowship hall on the right—same room as the baby shower where he'd first seen Jillian again. He set his salad on the long table in front near the kitchen. Two rectangular tables stretched part way across the center of the room. He caught his breath. The seat next to Jillian was empty.

After the tense moment they'd shared at the hospital, Riley wondered if she'd feel like talking to him. The worse she could do was move.

He poked his hands in his pocket, took a deep breath, and strolled toward the table. "Hey."

Jillian looked up at him.

Was it his imagination? Did her eyes brighten? Her smile widen? *Nah. I'm dreaming. She's dating that other guy.*

"Hey, Riley."

"When we go through the line, I need for you to take some of my potato salad and make sure it's fit for human consumption." He slipped down in the folding chair next to her. "I haven't made this since…" Riley's face warmed. He didn't want to inform the entire crowd of what he almost said. Before he went to prison. "I mean for a long time."

She patted his arm and grinned. "Well, I'm impressed you made the attempt. My cooking skills aren't the best either. That fruit plate will have to do."

One of the leaders stood near the food table. "Welcome everyone. Thank you all for coming. I'm sure we all took the calories out of these delicious dishes. Let's pray so we can eat."

What a contrast to his former life, praying before a meal. Quite a change from partying, drinking and drugs, to a church potluck.

The leader bowed his head. "Lord, thank You for this food and bless it to our nourishment. We pray Your name will be glorified through our fellowship tonight. Amen."

They went through the line, then Riley set his plate on the table next to Jillian's. *Hmm.* The enchilada casserole, the squash and cheese dish, salad, rolls, and rice made his stomach growl. He'd have to go back for the marinated beef and the green beans. Who said singles couldn't cook?

After the meal, the volunteer brought encouragement from the Word.

Riley soaked it in as if he'd never heard the message before. *Why couldn't this last all night?*

The leader closed his Bible after his final prayer. "Okay, people. Have a blessed rest of the evening."

Jillian stretched her arms in front of her, gathered her purse, and slipped the strap on her shoulder. When she turned to him with a smile, his pulse beat a little harder, reminding him of his growing feelings for her.

The situation with Jamie had created a bond between them though he hadn't realized it until now. He admired Jillian. From all he'd observed, she longed to see girls like Jamie come to the Lord and give their babies a chance at life. Or better yet, live by God's standards of behavior in the first place.

His pulse tripped again as he couldn't resist memorizing the shape of her eyes and the curve of her nose. Was it because of their ministry relationship or because he was falling in love with her, or both?

Riley grabbed their paper plates, dumped them in the garbage, and retrieved his empty bowl.

"It looks like your dish passed the test." She laughed and picked up a plastic tray from the serving table.

Inching his thumbs around the rim of the empty bowl, he sealed the lid and smirked. "No one seems to have food poisoning yet."

The cool June night swept across his face as they exited through the main doors. With a hard swallow, he summoned his nerve. "Hey, Jillian. Do you have plans right now? I need to make a trip to the animal shelter. Got the call this morning. They approved my application for a dog."

"What?" She took a step back on the pavement.

He cleared his throat. "Yeah, the pet adoption center. It's open late on Wednesdays. Could you...go with me to pick up my dog and help me get him settled in?" *Okay, now she probably thinks I've lost my mind.*

The sparkle in her eyes stoked his elevated pulse higher. "Sure, but I don't know too much about dogs."

"That's okay. Just go with me." Riley explored her aquamarine eyes, her graceful chin and the curve of her neck. Yeah, he wanted her to go along. But he had to admit, this was another excuse to enjoy her company.

~

Riley propped the metal door open with his shoulder and held his hand out to Jillian. He recoiled as the scent of wet dog hit him when he followed her into the pet shelter. Not unpleasant, merely...distinctive, especially with the underlying odor of medicated shampoo. Yapping sounds came from the back.

The same young woman as the last time he'd been there manned the counter tonight. "Hello. How may I help you?"

A framed newspaper article featuring the shelter hung on the wall over a metal desk. A picture of a mixed breed mutt with the name *Lucky* underneath rested in a white frame on one side of the counter. Riley nodded. "I've come to pick up my dog. Riley Mathis. You approved my paperwork."

The worker perused her computer screen. "Yes, I see it here. You had asked for a breed that would make a good watch dog." She pointed toward the back where Riley had heard the noisy barks on his first visit. "The attendant can assist you."

"Thank you." He gave Jillian a smile. "Ready?"

"Sure, but I'm curious." Jillian peered at him. "Why do you want a watchdog?"

Riley's shoulders tensed. She would have to ask that question. He couldn't tell her he expected his old cellmate to return. That James might even break in for a little revenge. A barking dog made a good deterrent and would scare him off. "Oh, I...uh, it never hurts to have a noisy dog around the house. You know, man's best friend."

"If I didn't live on the fifth floor of Rainier Regency, I might get one, too." She followed him back to the kennels.

The canine chorus intensified when he opened the door, making him chuckle. A series of wire cages were stacked two high on the right side of the wall. A sleeping bulldog puppy lay on an old gray blanket in the first cage. On top, some type of a terrier with one black eye chewed on a piece of an old towel.

They strolled past a few cages that held mongrels. "I've heard mixed breed dogs are very smart, and sometimes more trainable than a purebred. I'm kind of glad I chose a mutt."

In the top cage at the end of the row, Riley's medium-sized Labrador stretched out his front paws and whined. He raised his curly Chow-like tail over his body. His head looked like a German Shepherd's. Yep, definitely a mutt.

When he stuck his finger through the slot, the dog gave him a lick. The little creature wagged its tail so fast, Riley feared it might fall off. "What do you think about him?"

Jillian poked her finger through the cage, and the

dog *kissed* her finger, too. "He's adorable."

A chubby man wearing an apron ambled toward them. "Here to take your dog home?"

"Yes. My paper work was approved after we talked last time."

"Well, you made a good selection. He's house trained and has all his shots. And he has a protective nature, like we talked about."

The dog panted, tongue lolling and lips curled back.

"No way." Riley laughed. "Did you see that? I think he's smiling."

Jillian placed the back of her hand on Riley's forehead. "It's a good thing I'm a doctor. Are you sure you're okay? I don't think dogs know how to smile."

He couldn't restrain the colossal grin on his face. "Well, this one did."

Arms folded over her chest, she raised an eyebrow. "This dog looks too cute to be a watchdog. You want one that's scary looking."

The attendant retied his apron. "Ma'am. Sam's a mixed breed. He's friendly because of the Labrador in him, but his German Shepherd blood should make him a good guard dog."

Jillian stroked Sam's furry head with two fingers through the bars. "I like him."

Sam gave an excited yelp.

This little mutt had caught Riley's attention from the first. He stuck his hands in his pockets. With a glance toward the attendant, he nodded. "I'm ready to pay."

"Okay. I'm sure you won't be sorry." He unlocked the cage and reached for Sam.

The dog yapped and curled his lips again, making Riley laugh.

The worker picked Sam up. "Come here, fellow." He moved toward the door to the office.

Though Riley wanted to carry the dog out, he would wait a little longer. He resisted humming the tune "How Much Is That Doggie in the Window" that his mom used to sing.

Jillian grinned at him and gave him a thumbs up.

"I have an old collar and leash someone left. You can use it if you'd like." The attendant strolled toward the woman behind the desk. "We're all set here." He picked up the collar hanging on a hook and placed it over Sam's head, tightening the clasp a little. Then he attached the leash and handed the loop to Jillian.

Sam showed no resistance, instead wagged his tail.

Riley handed the clerk the credit card Dexter helped him get.

When she finished the transaction, Riley looked down at Sam curling up against Jillian's leg. "Okay, little dog. We're ready to go."

Wrapping the end of the leash around her arm a couple of times, Jillian ran her fingers over Sam's collar.

The little dog pranced out to the curb as if he knew exactly where he was headed.

With a giggle, Jillian grinned. "He can sit on my lap."

Riley's mouth gaped open. He threw his head back with a laugh and grasped the leash. "Uh, Jillian. They did promise he was house trained. Do we trust their word?"

She slipped into the passenger's side and patted her legs. "Just put him here. I'm not worried."

Lifting the dog onto her lap, he handed her the end

of the leash. "Now, I hope he's going to like his new home."

~

Jillian couldn't move from the small sofa. Every time she tried, Riley's little dog whined and made a few circles on the couch beside her. Sam had a full stomach now, had drunk plenty of water, and made a successful trip outside to Riley's backyard. He probably wanted to take a nap and enjoyed the warmth of her body—kinda like a mommy. He just needed a little TLC, poor baby.

When she trailed her hand down his blond fur, Sam licked her palm and nestled beside her once again.

"I think you've made a friend for life." Riley eased down on the couch next to her. "I can't thank you enough for your help."

"I think he likes me." Jillian scratched the dog behind his ears. "What do you think about his name, Sam?"

Riley circled his finger on top of the dog's head. "Since I need a strong watchdog, Sam seems like a good name because it reminds me of Samson, from the Bible."

"I'd agree, but he's going to have to grow a little more before he looks fierce." Jillian leaned her head back against the couch pillow. Sitting here with Riley seemed so right, the bustle and stress of the hospital eons away. She drew her hand along Samson's fur and released a deep sigh.

"I'm thinking you're right. But I bet he'll let me know when someone comes to the door, even if he's still a little guy." Riley reached toward Samson to stroke his fur and brushed her hand. When her gaze locked on him, he kept eye contact a moment then averted his focus to Samson. "Jillian, I... I..."

What was he trying to say? Did he want to ask her if she had feelings for him?

How *did* she feel about him? *He's an ex-con.* She was practically engaged to someone else, an accomplished doctor. She'd be foolish to fall for Riley.

Jillian studied his electric blue eyes. Desire to feel his lips on hers and melt into his arms canceled any more objections she held. She had to admit the truth. Riley had stolen her heart. She relaxed into the couch cushions. The warmth of his large hand covering hers filled her with peace.

He leaned toward her and slipped an arm around the back of the couch. His face, inches away, peered at her as if trying to discover the answer to a question. "Jillian, can I...do you mind if..." He ran his finger over her palm and trailed it up her arm.

He didn't have to speak the words. She read them on his face, in his eyes, and on his mouth. *He wants to kiss me.* She touched his prickly cheek. "I want it, too."

For a moment longer he gazed at her, then closed his eyes. His lips brushed her cheek and paused on her mouth, moving quietly over her lips, not in the demanding way Jett kissed her. When he nibbled the skin behind her ear, her breath caught in her chest. His lips sent fulfillment to a place deep inside her.

A recollection slid across her memory. His kiss, so like another.

Riley gave her the masculine attention she craved, but tonight went far beyond that. He stirred her in a way Jett never had. Riley not only ignited a fire in her, but he made her feel valuable and respected. A contented sigh escaped her throat.

His eyes narrowed to slits. He ran his thumb from her jaw down her neck. When his arm slipped around her shoulders and pulled her closer, Samson whimpered and nuzzled his head into her lap.

"Jillian." Riley's whispered words stole her breath. "I know I'm not the kind of man you'd choose. I wish it weren't so, but I can't get you out of my mind…or my heart."

Chapter Sixteen

Sunshine streamed in through the long windows. If Jillian didn't have another patient, she'd change into shorts and leave for a jog in the park. The stairwell to her left would take her to the cafeteria quicker than the elevator. Besides, she needed the exercise and a distraction from her thoughts of Riley.

She stepped onto the landing for the first floor and continued down to the basement. Her solid grasp on the handrails steadied her. If only her relationship with men was as firm.

If she had the chance, she'd asked Riley what he meant the night he kissed her. He cared for her but wished it weren't so. Was that good or bad? She chewed the nail of her little finger.

Ten more steps to the basement and the cafeteria down the hall. What about Jett? He'd proposed and said he'd have her ring soon. Jillian was almost an engaged woman. If she were honest, she hadn't made up her mind. Was she in love with him? His successful career and good looks tempted her, but...

Riley had come to mean more to her than she'd realized. Their first kiss, though brief, had thrilled her. She could've kissed him back with even more passion.

Thinking about his lips brushing her cheek caused her head to swim. He made her heart pound like no man had ever done before.

But what about his prison record? She gave herself a mental kick. In God's sight, they were both guilty of wrongdoing. The Lord had forgiven her and Riley for the past. He was a brother in Christ. That was all that mattered.

She pushed open the door from the stairwell with more force than she intended. *Okay, face it. I have feelings for Riley, but any sane person would advise me to choose Jett.* Jillian squeezed her eyes shut, but when she opened them again the frustration inside still churned. *Riley, why did I have to fall in love with you?*

A cup of coffee might help. The hot, dark liquid always boosted her outlook. She filled a Styrofoam cup from the coffee urn spigot on the line and paid the cashier. An open table sat toward the window in the back of the room.

"Jillian, over here."

She looked up.

"Hey, gorgeous." Jett waved at her from a table near the wall. "How's your morning going?" He stood and slid a chair out for her.

Why did she have to contend with him right now? She needed more time to think, to get things resolved in her mind. "Going well. I'm heading to the clinic as soon as I finish up here." Jillian set her cup on the table and folded her fingers.

"I'd planned to text you later to see if you wanted to go to dinner with me." Jett covered her hands with his and searched her face.

Less than twenty-four hours ago, another large hand

had covered hers. But this time her heart remained lodged inside her chest instead of floating away on a winding river of desire.

Jett reached into his trouser pocket. "I guess now is as good as any time to give this to you." He pulled out a small black box and opened it. A sparking diamond, at least two carats in size, twinkled at her.

She widened her eyes. Jett hadn't skimped on the stunning gem. "I can't believe this." How could he want to give it to her here in the hospital cafeteria, the least romantic place she could think of? She sucked in a breath. Was the man so centered on his work that he couldn't think of a romantic setting?

He offered her a half-grin. "I can see by the expression on your face you're impressed. Jett Camp doesn't skimp on anything. Nothing but the best for you."

How could he have so completely misinterpreted her reaction? Didn't he know her at all? Yes, the ring was exquisite, but she couldn't take it yet. Not here, and not with her feelings for Riley. If she could stall Jett for a while, perhaps she'd come to her senses and forget about Riley Mathis. "This is very sweet of you, but we're in the hospital cafeteria. Let's wait for another time."

Jett raised an eyebrow, gave a huff, and snapped the box shut. "I think most any woman would be happy to get a ring like this no matter where they were. You'll have to let me know when you're ready. I'm not going to beg you." The tight inflection of his low-pitched baritone sent a chill down her spine. He narrowed his eyes, stuffed the ring back in his pocket, screeched his chair back, and marched toward the exit.

A ring was something Jillian had dreamed of for so long. If she were to guess, Jett meant to intimidate her with his performance, hoping she'd beg him to come back. But a strange calm filtered through her. His display of temper hadn't affected her at all.

~

Riley craned his neck to peer at every corner of the waiting room. Jillian had said to meet her here. Something about Jamie, that she might want to see them both. Maybe because they spoke to her that day at Waterfall Park. He cracked his knuckles and settled back in the vinyl chair.

He resisted the urge to dust and empty the garbage, but his shift didn't start until later. What about when he finished his education and became a successful accountant? Would he still want to vacuum the floors and straighten the magazines? He chuckled at the idea.

The thought of Jillian's presence both exhilarated him and made him nervous. He fidgeted in his chair. Her aquamarine eyes, tall frame, and womanly curves took his breath away. He sat up straight and ran a hand through his hair. He had it bad.

She'd wanted his kiss. But after thinking about it, did she regret it?

"Beautiful Things" sounded in Riley's pocket. When he fished his phone out, he glanced at the caller ID. "Hey, Jillian."

"Riley, can you come down to Jamie's room? She's in 214."

Riley tensed his shoulders. At least she didn't sound panicked this time. "Sure, I'm on my way." Her voice revealed nothing. Maybe good news awaited him.

He headed down the hall, tapped on the door, and pushed a smile in place when he walked in.

With a hand on Jamie's shoulder, Jillian sat in a chair by her bed.

He caught his breath at the sight of Jillian. Was it because of her concern or her dress that fit close to her body and matched her eyes? A frown marred her brow.

Tension filled the room like a tangible thing. His smile faded.

Jillian looked up to him with a weak smile. "Jamie asked for you, too. Since you were there that day in the park. She's grateful you tried to help her."

The tears Jamie allowed to roll down her cheeks moistened her pillow. She moved a tortured gaze from him to Jillian.

Riley pulled up a chair at the end of the bed and stretched his neck from one side to the other. He hadn't dealt with many crying girls, though he'd held Jillian the day she'd wept over Jamie. Could he find words of consolation? All he knew was to share about God's power in changing a person's life.

When Jillian patted Jamie's hand, he couldn't hear her whispered words. The teen's sobs seemed endless.

Nothing to do but pray for her. Riley closed his eyes and covered his face with his hands. When he heard Jamie take a heaving breath, he looked toward her again.

"I feel so empty. I never thought I would care about the unborn life I destroyed." Jamie gave another sob.

"It's like a chasm." Jillian ran her fingers over Jamie's hand. "One so deep you don't know if you'll ever be able to pour enough love into it to make you whole again."

"How do you know? How could you possibly understand what it feels like?" Jamie covered her face.

Jillian cleared her throat and began the story Riley knew so well, the tale that had tormented him day after day since she'd come back into his life, the truth that gouged his heart out. But he couldn't change it.

With heavy steps, he plodded to the entrance of the hospital room, staring out the glass window in the door. Could he bear to hear her speak of her pain again? Every tear that rolled down her cheek felt like acid burning a hole in him. If only he had an undo button for his life, like on his computer. But even if he could go back, would he get it right the second time? He'd been so stupid and young, so full of himself.

Please Lord, show me how to make this up to her. He forced himself to face Jillian and watch her tormented look as she finished the story.

A soft sob tore from her throat. "I made the decision to abort my baby, and I couldn't turn back. I thought I had no other option." Jillian paused, took a deep breath, and dabbed at her eyes with a tissue. "My parents would've been so disappointed if they'd known the truth. At the time, I believed I'd never be able to go to college, let alone med school." Her shoulders fell forward. "I still think about the man who did this to me, yet I couldn't pick him out of a lineup if I had to. I was too wasted."

The man who did that to her. *Dear God. That man is me.* Riley's lack of responsibility, his failures in college, and his selfishness smacked him in his forehead. *Others suffer from our mistakes.* Jillian, his child, not to mention his mom, who'd lost a grandchild.

"I often wonder about him, Jamie. If he knew I carried his child, would he have tried to talk me out of taking its life?"

Jillian's words seared him. Riley clamped his lips shut.

He took a few steps toward Jamie and patted her shoulder. Remorse pervaded his soul with an ache that hurt worse than any beating he'd ever taken in prison. "I'm praying for you, Jamie. But I want you to know, I understand how you feel, how both of you feel."

With wide eyes, Jillian turned to him.

Jamie frowned. "You?" She snorted. "I doubt it. How could you possibly know what we lost?"

"I understand your feelings because..." The door sat ajar, and he pushed it shut. He'd almost said because I lost a lost a child as well, the child that Jillian had carried. "Because I lost...my father, and I remember the emptiness afterwards." Though he spoke the truth, the sting of losing their child hurt too, but in a different way.

Dread filled his emotions. The time had finally come. He had to tell Jillian the truth, but not here, not in front of Jamie.

He couldn't act like a coward any longer, unaccountable to the woman he loved. "But if I...had been the one responsible for getting a girl pregnant, I would feel the guilt and pain now, every bit as much as you." He caught Jillian's gaze and didn't let go. "As a man, I would grieve knowing I took advantage of her. I would understand the value of what she gave me, and how I robbed her of something only a loving husband deserved." The words tumbled out all in one breath as the volume of his voice rose. "Yeah, I'd feel the emptiness inside me, too." He forced back a tear that threatened.

Jillian's face turned ashen as she stared at him. Had she comprehended the meaning behind his words?

Riley rose from the chair. "I'll leave you two alone now." He stumbled toward the door and stopped. "Jillian, I'd like to talk to you when you finish up here. Could you meet me in the hospital gardens?"

She gave him a torturous glance and cleared her throat. "All right."

Riley staggered down the hall. This might be the last day he'd converse with the woman he loved so dearly.

~

Jillian summoned every bit of control she had. She couldn't show Jamie the mix of emotions threatening to collide. She regarded the girl as a mother would, yet Jamie was still her patient. Jillian tucked the covers around her and brushed a strand of hair away from her face.

"Thank you. I feel better now." Jamie's lips formed a wan smile. "I'm glad both of you were here."

Jillian would never forget Riley's presence tonight. "God loves you, Jamie, and so do I." She gave her a light kiss on her forehead. "We're friends, right?"

Jamie nodded. She paused, peering at Jillian. The teen grasped her arm. "You know, somehow I think Riley does know how it feels to suffer loss."

Had Jamie perceived his message, too? Jillian's lips trembled. She couldn't talk to the girl about Riley. The bottom had fallen out of her world. The man she loved had deceived her. *Get out of the room.* The words warned and yelled from within.

Her patient squeezed harder. "Jillian, I think he cares about you. I saw it in his face."

Tears badgered Jillian, looming at the back of her eyes. She could never admit the truth to Jamie. "I don't think so."

"Listen to me. Love him, okay? He looks like he could use it."

Jillian had to change the focus of the conversation before she blurted out what she'd learned. "Are you still interested in going to church with me?"

"More than anything."

Jillian forced a smile to her lips. "I'll visit you tomorrow before you're released, and we'll make plans for you to attend on Sunday." She kissed her two fingers and placed them on Jamie's forehead before walking out of the room.

As she tromped down the hall, an arctic freeze began at her toes and crept up her body. Her heart pounded. Outside Jamie's room, she could face the truth. She'd well understood the message Riley cast upon her.

Jillian shook her head. Now that she thought of it, the signs were there, if she had only taken the time to see them. The first day she met up with Riley in the park, the way he'd held his shoulders seemed familiar. The night he kissed her with such tenderness, she'd recalled the same gentle affection the college boy had shown her. Riley Mathis was the same person from so long ago, the father of her baby.

~

The moonlight sparkled on the path to the garden bench, mocking her. A romantic backdrop, a place for lovers. Great heaving sobs escaped her throat like a swollen river finally releasing a torrent of water downstream. She clutched the sapphire necklace under her tee shirt. *That's it.* He hadn't ogled her chest the first day they met again. He'd stared at her jewelry. The treasure Grandmother had given her. Remembered her from that night. Jillian grasped the trunk of a tree as a dizzy ripple cavorted through her head threatening her balance.

How dare he? Riley had deceived her. Rage filled her, boiling up from her soul. He had the nerve to hang around her all these weeks and not tell her.

He sat on the garden bench, his head in his hands. "Dear Lord, let her forgive me. Please let her forgive me."

Jillian slid down on the other end of the bench. Her knees shook. "Riley. Why didn't you tell me before?" A low moan filled with agony climbed up her throat. She clenched her jaw, fighting for control.

He'd mocked her and violated her that night, but he'd made it worse by not telling her who he was when they'd met again. Silent sobs shook her shoulders. "God, You say to forgive, but I can't. I'll never excuse him."

A warm arm slid around her. Through her tears, a blurry image of Riley loomed in front of her. She jerked away.

"I am so, so sorry, Jillian. I was a coward, a fool for keeping the truth from you." He reached toward her to push a strand of hair out of her eyes.

"Leave me alone." Jillian shoved his hand away. "I never want to see you again."

Tortured eyes stared at her. "Please forgive me." His words were barely a whisper, a soft, low cry.

She couldn't trust Riley now any more than she could ten years ago. With a hand to her throat, Jillian stood and glared at him. "Never, never speak to me again."

JUNE FOSTER

Chapter Seventeen

The modest red brick house brought mixed emotion after living there alone for years with Mom when Dad died. Then Dexter arrived in their lives. Things hadn't gotten any better. Tension stiffened Riley's shoulders and traveled all the way down to his toes.

Sam whined from his little cage in the back seat. Maybe this wasn't such a good idea after all. But almost like a proud papa, he wanted to show Mom his dog, the recipient of her generous donations.

With a few wiggles, Sam crawled out of his cage when Riley opened the latch. "Come here, little fellow. You're going to meet your grandma." Riley's smile faded. Because of his stupid actions, Mom had a grandchild for real, though she'd never held the infant in her arms.

Riley slipped the leash on Sam's collar and took a few hesitant steps up the sidewalk. "Sam, mind your manners when we get inside."

Sam curled his lips and wagged his curly tail as he bounded past Mom's roses bushes toward the front door.

Riley tapped and pushed the door ajar. "Mom, I've

got someone for you to meet." He reached down to Sam, took off the lease, and picked him up.

Mom dried her hands on her apron and walked through the living room. A huge grin crossed her face when she spied Sam. She held out her arms. "Well, hello, there." She glanced from Sam to Riley and gave him a kiss on his cheek.

"I'm not going to stay long. I just wanted you to meet Sam." He held the dog in his grip, not wanting him to get into any mischief, like tearing up one of the kids' toys or making a puddle on the floor. Since Sam hadn't had any accidents so far, Riley doubted he would here. Still, he played it safe.

"Oh, he looks like a good little puppy." Mom took Sam in her arms and sat down on the couch. She patted the spot next to her. "Sit down, honey. You know you're welcome anytime."

Emotion stung the back of his eyes. His Mom loved and accepted him no matter what he'd done. Almost like God's love. He prayed someday he could be an actual father to a child, nurturing him or her in the same way, showing them how valuable they were in God's eyes and to him.

With a quiet whimper. Sam curled up on Mom's lap.

She stroked his fur and giggled when he licked her hand. "He's adorable."

Riley stretched his feet out and put his hands behind his head. For a fleeting second, he thought of telling Mom about Jillian. *No*. He was an adult. He couldn't go around crying on his mommy's shoulder.

But if Jillian had only returned his phone messages and hadn't ignored him in the hall at the hospital when he swept the floors, he might not feel as bad. When he thought about it, he didn't blame her, but if they could make peace and part friends, that would be all he'd ask.

Riley scanned the room. "How are the kids doing?" Anything to get his mind off Jillian, though he did care about the children.

Mom pointed to the little baby bed near the door that led to the hall. "I've been pretty busy with this new little baby girl. The other kids are in school right now."

Riley's heart warmed. "I really admire you for what you do."

She gave him a pat on his cheek. "It's one way I can serve the Lord."

When the newborn gurgled, Riley pushed up from the couch and took a few steps toward the baby.

The tiny features of her little face were perfect. A shock of fuzzy blond hair peeked out from the blanket. He hadn't realized infants were so small. "How long will you have the baby?" He walked back to the couch and sat down.

"You know how it goes. The court system moves slower than a giant tortoise." She gave Sam another pat. "Son, how are you...really?"

Did his demeanor reveal that much about him, or was Mom an expert at reading his feelings? "Oh, fine. I guess I could use some prayer. You know, for work and school." *And because the woman I love walked out of my life.* Riley hung his head and studied the rough calluses on his hands.

Her eyes narrowed, yet the expression on her face sent peace to his soul. "Let's ask God right now to help you." Mom grasped his hand. "Dear Lord…"

The sound of the doorbell circulated through the room. Sam jumped out of her lap onto the floor next to the couch.

"Excuse me, honey." She stood and glanced at her watch. "Oh, I forgot." She tapped her head. "I've got an appointment at two. I met a young doctor who's interested in beginning a clinic for pregnant teens. She wants to learn about the Foster-care system." Mom strolled to the door with a glance toward him. "I'm sorry, Riley. This shouldn't take too long. We'll pray after she leaves."

Riley stiffened. A young doctor wanting to start a clinic? Jillian. It had to be her.

Mom smoothed her shirt and pulled open the door. "Come in, Dr. Coleman." His mother stepped aside so Jillian could enter the room.

Like a little kid caught stealing from his mother's purse, heat began in his cheeks and careened down his chest. He wanted to escape, but there was no way to exit unnoticed.

His mother waved toward Riley. "This is my son, Riley Mathis."

Jillian's smile faded as her eyes widened. "Oh…oh, yes." She cleared her throat. "We've already met. He goes to…uh, my church."

"Yeah. Hi." Her last words echoed in his memory. *Never speak to me again.* He had to get out of there. *Now.*

Jillian looked frantic, searching the room as if contemplating an escape route.

Sam gave a yip and bounded toward her, his tail wagging so fast, Riley thought he'd take off in flight.

Jillian gave Riley a tormented look, then glanced down at the dog. "Hi, Sam."

Riley rushed toward the puppy, now jumping up on

Jillian. "Come here, you bad boy. This lady doesn't want you pestering her." He scooped his dog up in his arms, picked up the leash from the floor, and started toward the door. He curved around to his Mom. "Catch you next time."

~

Jillian's tense muscles hadn't relaxed. Seeing Riley and Sam tore at a place in her heart, bringing memories of the night when Riley kissed her and Sam snuggled in her lap. The little puppy had remembered her.

"You know the dog's name?" Marion gazed at her.

"Yes, I think Riley must've mentioned it or something." Jillian bit her lip.

"Oh, I see."

Her gracious smile set Jillian at ease.

"Please, sit down." She held her hand out to the easy chair across from the couch. "Oh, and excuse me a moment. I need to wash my hands. I've been petting my little granddog." Marion turned around toward the kitchen behind a long couch.

Marion's granddog. Jillian caught her breath. The kind woman had more than a grand dog. Jillian had once carried her grandchild.

Marion returned to the living room rubbing her hands together. "There, now."

Jillian attempted to relax her shoulders. "Well, Marion. I certainly appreciate your help."

"I'll be happy to answer any questions you have." She strolled to the bassinette. "First I'd like to introduce you to the latest little visitor to our home." She picked up the baby and neared Jillian in the beige chair.

"Would you like to hold her, dear?"

Jillian sucked in a breath and held out her arms. "Oh, Marion. She's so precious. She must be about a week old."

"Yes, exactly." Marion placed the baby in Jillian's hold.

She cradled the child, a tiny helpless life. As a doctor, she dealt with newborns daily, but this infant made her pulse thud in her chest. Even though the mother didn't keep her, she'd allowed the child to live. Jillian held her breath, trying to keep her emotions inside, where they belonged. "Thank you so much for inviting me into your home."

If Jillian could get past the surprise and unease of the last half hour, she'd be thankful. Seeing Riley was tough. To sit with him in his mother's living room as if they had never conceived a child together, trying to deny she loved him, and not trusting him enough to forgive him tortured her. "Now, I need an idea of some of the responsibilities required of you on a daily basis. I mean, examples of things you do to provide for the children's needs."

The baby stretched one little arm out from the blanket.

"Well, dear. Of course we supply their physical needs—healthful, nutritious meals. We see they are properly clothed and help them attain good hygiene skills."

Jillian peered at Marion, barely hearing her words. She glanced at the mantel over the fireplace. A picture of a younger Riley sat on the shelf. Is that how he looked the night they...? "Uh, Marion, what about doctor appointments and medication?"

Riley's mother searched her face. Did she have any idea what lay between her son and Jillian? Surely not.

"Oh, the initial medical assessments are included in the court-approved social services plan. I'm responsible for transporting the children to all their appointments and picking up their meds."

"I...uh..." Jillian had another question, but the picture on the mantel demanded one more glance.

Marion rose to her feet and took the baby from Jillian's arms and returned her to the bassinette. Then she retrieved the frame from the mantel. "This is Riley, in college. My boy has changed so much since then." Marion's eyes danced with the light of the sun shining in the window.

"Yes, he does look different now than in that picture. More mature. But then, he's ten years older." She supposed the free-spirited Riley Mathis from college had changed. After all, he'd become a Christian.

Marion held the frame to her chest, glanced at it again with adoring eyes, and replaced it on the bookshelf.

Jillian bounced to her feet. She had to leave. Though Marion's kind nature put her at ease at first, Jillian could no longer remain in the room with Riley's picture, the young man who took her upstairs that night.

Though the image of his presence disturbed her, it also taunted her. She was repelled by the young Riley but at the same time, drawn in by those same electric-blue eyes that sent a thrill down her spine, even now—even after their last encounter.

Chapter Eighteen

Jillian wandered through the lobby and past the wall with *Rainier Regency* written in gold letters. She pushed open the double doors at the back of the building and followed the path to the adult pool. Finally, a sunny day. She scooted a reclining chair away from the pool, hoping to deflect any splashes that came her way. Maybe she'd swim later in the afternoon after she read a little more of her book *Hungry for Love, a Christian Woman's Perspective.*

The first part of the title still made her uncomfortable. Hungry for love? *Yes*. She hadn't wanted to admit it at first, but Dad's emotional distance since childhood had impacted her. Since her early teens, she'd searched for a man who could fill that basic void in her life. A good thing no one was around to witness her face, which must've turned bright red if the perspiration was any indication.

Riley had used her, but in a sense she'd used him too—to provide the love she so desperately needed. She gripped the recliner's metal arms. If he'd told her the truth from the start, she might have forgiven him. But now? She couldn't tolerate a relationship that formed under a shroud of poor communication and secrets.

She flipped her sunglasses up on her nose, leaned back onto the cushions of the recliner, and closed her eyes. The sounds of laughter and splashing water met her ears. Some guy and a girl, probably infatuated with each other.

More like a huff, she exhaled a frustrated breath. Riley's face dominated her mind without asking permission, his light brown hair parted in the middle, his captivating blue eyes and lips that turned up at the edges as if he had the answer to an intriguing mystery. How many times had she wanted to run her finger down the light stubble on his face? Wrap her arms around his wide shoulders? His lips on…

A breeze whisked a strand of hair from her face, and she bolted up. What was she doing? Dreaming about how it would feel if he kissed her. She had to be honest about her feelings. One minute she loved him, and the next she was angry. Jillian yanked a strand of hair and squeezed. Her thoughts about Riley were as confusing as learning a new language.

"Hello, Ms. Gorgeous Lady. I knocked on your door. When you didn't answer, I figured you'd be out here getting some sun."

Whipping off her sunglasses, she glanced up.

Jett pulled up a recliner and sat down. His black sports shirt he'd buttoned halfway up made his blond hair even lighter, like a field of daffodils.

Instead of looking into his intense blue eyes, she studied her hands, gripped in her lap. The last time she'd spoken with him, they parted under less than pleasant terms. "When we talked at the hospital, you were kinda mad at me."

"I know." He took her hand. "But every time I think

about you, my heart tells me I can't let you get away." He drew her hand to his chest. "I really do care about you. I love you, but I don't need an ultrasound machine to fall on me to figure out something is coming between us."

Jillian's mouth dropped open. She snapped it shut. He loved her? She supposed she never really thought he did. He certainly hadn't said so. Until now she'd believed he found it convenient to have a relationship with someone who understood his profession and its demands.

"Oh, Jett, it's just that…" She wanted to tell him about the abortion, about Riley, but she couldn't. He wouldn't understand her sense of guilt. Even as a doctor, he didn't value life the way she did. She shook her head. "There's nothing the matter."

The black box made an appearance again when Jett reached into his pocket with his other hand and pulled out the velvet container. Dropping her hand, he opened the lid and lifted the ring from the black velvet slot. Then he grasped her left finger.

"Jett, not now." Jillian jerked her hand away. "I can't at this moment. I'm sorry." Riley had kept the truth from her. Now she'd done the same with Jett. She couldn't accept his ring until she had the courage to tell him the truth about her past, despite knowing what his reaction would be.

~

Riley maneuvered his car around the concrete divisions of the hospital's massive parking lot. Up past the evergreen tree about one hundred yards away, a van pulled out. Finally a place about a half block from the entrance.

Though he missed Jillian terribly, he needed to focus on the positives. Thank the Lord for the extra hours Dexter had given him. Less time to dream about the woman who'd captured his heart, and at the same time more opportunity to earn money for college.

Poking along past the cars to the open parking space, Riley scratched his head. His stepfather must be pleased. There'd been no complaints from clients lately.

Maybe Dexter would notice Riley no longer took the shortcuts. More than anything, he needed to prove his responsibility to his family, to the people he'd disappointed all those years ago.

But with Jillian, he'd never have that chance now.

The van finally backed out. Riley parked, turned off the ignition, and picked up the documents Dexter asked him to deliver to the administration office.

At the information desk, a sign said Woodlyn Hospital Business Office and pointed to the left. Riley trudged down the hall to the third door on the right. After leaving the folder with the smiling young attendant, he walked down the hall again and out the main entrance.

He drew his shoulders back and allowed a new sense of pride to elevate his low self-image. Dexter wanted him to return to the main office and begin learning some of the paper work. Guess he figured Riley might be able to take over the books one of these days as his college classes progressed.

Though he didn't feel as chipper as he'd like, he puckered his lips and whistled "Amazing Grace." The sidewalk from the entrance led to the vast parking lot.

He sucked in a sharp breath, but resisted the urge to turn around and scoot inside the building. Jillian and Dr. Camp strode toward him not more than fifty yards away from the doctors' parking lot. Jillian said something to Dr. Camp and looked up. She'd seen him.

No way could he avoid them now. Even if he did turn around, Jillian would know. Maybe if he pretended to study the pavement, they'd walk right by.

Though he wanted to keep his focus averted, a force beyond his own will lifted his gaze. His pulse pounded as he made eye contact with Jillian.

Dr. Camp glanced at Riley, turned his head to stare at Jillian's tortured expression, and pressed his lips together. "He's the reason, isn't he?"

The pit of Riley's stomach wrenched. He fought a wave of nausea. What did the doctor mean? No other explanation except that Jillian must've told him everything.

Riley's feet adhered to the pavement. The couple stood not more than a couple of yards in front of him. He had to face whatever came next.

The doctor marched toward him, lifted his fist shoulder height, and slugged Riley's jaw.

Before he knew what happened, he lay on his backside on the payment. He sat up and rubbed his cheek as Camp stood over him shaking a fist.

"You lousy, no-good excuse for a man. You can't even get up and fight." Camp bared his teeth and snarled at him.

In prison, if an inmate hit him like that, he'd have been on his feet returning the blow. If you didn't stand your ground there, you died. But here, he knew the reason for the doctor's actions. He defended Jillian's honor, furious about what Riley had done to her.

He knew the best thing to do. Not fight back. What was the point? Jillian's boyfriend was right. Riley rubbed his jaw again and stood.

Jett dropped his fists, frowned, and rubbed his hand over his mouth.

Jillian stared at them open-mouthed, clutched her briefcase, and stormed toward the main entrance of the hospital, the heels of her shoes clacking against the concrete.

Dr. Camp gawked at her and scowled at Riley. After the doctor crawled into his Infinity in the doctor's section, he slammed the door. When he reached the main road in front of the hospital, he gunned his motor and sped away, disappearing around the corner.

Something warm trickled down Riley's face, from his nose to his chin. He wiped his hand over his mouth and held it out in front of him. Blood. As he stumbled to his car a half block away, he swiped at his nose with his sleeve.

The glove compartment contained a few napkins he'd saved from Chick-fil-A. Glancing between the rearview mirror and the road, he used them to clean his face. To go home and change first might be a wise idea, but Dexter expected him back right away. The blood on his face had dried.

What if he called his boss and told him he'd been held up in traffic? No, the streets weren't crowded this time of day. Couldn't have his stepfather thinking he had been wasting time. Instead he'd wash up in the bathroom at the office before he ever saw him.

He snapped his fingers. An extra work shirt with Woodlyn Building Maintenance sewn on the front was in his locker. He'd clean up, put on a new shirt, and report to Dex. It wouldn't take long.

When he arrived in front of the office, he pushed the door open and darted toward the restroom and lockers in the back of the building.

Every muscle stiffened when he saw Dexter pushing an office vac toward the end of the shelving. He parked it against the wall, blocking the path. He looked up as Riley took a step toward him.

Dex stared a moment then shook his head. "I told Dr. Camp when he called a few minutes ago I didn't believe it, that you attacked him again. But your bloody face certainly indicates a confrontation. He said you deserved to be fired, and I'm wondering if I don't agree with him." Dexter ran a hand through his hair and took a few steps toward him. "The last time Dr. Camp said you assaulted him, it was because you were defending someone's honor. I was proud of you then. But now, this was an unprovoked act of violence. I can't have it. Riley, I've overlooked far too much now. I don't care if I'm married to your mother. You're fired."

Dexter's words hurt more than a blow to his gut. But Dr. Camp's lie caused him more pain than if he'd taken forty lashes with a horse-whip.

He hung his head and turned around to walk out the door. Guess his opportunity to take care of Woodlyn Maintenance books was short-lived.

Jillian could prove he'd been the one harmed, but even if she had a reason to talk to Dexter, she probably wouldn't come to Riley's defense. Not this time. She didn't care. And why should she? He was a lost cause.

Chapter Nineteen

Fired.

How would he pay his rent now? And what about class?

The knot in Riley's chest wound so tight he couldn't breathe. He'd never finish school at this rate, never rise above the stigma of prison. No one would hire a convicted felon. No one but Dexter, and he'd blown that opportunity.

The black thought tormented him. He couldn't stay with his mom while he searched for another job. Not with her running a foster care program in her home and with Dexter there. The authorities frowned on ex-cons hanging around kids. Maybe the YMCA. At least until they kicked him out, too. Which left the streets. He shuddered.

He'd blown it. His stepfather hadn't even given him a chance to explain. If he had, no way he'd have believed Riley didn't slug the doctor.

But Camp had a good reason to hit him. Now the doctor would always think of Riley as a wimp. But beyond that, Camp had created this lie and taken the extra step of calling Dexter. The man must really *hate* him.

With no one else to worry about, he could go get cleaned up now. He started his car and pulled out of the parking lot. At least he still had his own place for two more weeks.

What had he been thinking? A career as an accountant? He tapped his forehead with the heel of his hand. He'd been dreaming about the gorgeous doctor, of someday making a life with her. What a farce.

A fool. A ludicrous, preposterous fool. He'd screwed up his life ten years ago, and nothing could change that. Nothing would make any difference.

Instead of home, Riley pulled to the curb next to the park and slumped against his seat. A heavy sigh escaped, but it didn't help. Maybe he could find peace here. Cascade Waterfall Park, where his world tipped upside down. Though he'd been arrested here ten years ago, he now worked to save other kids from his mistakes.

The park ran two city blocks along Main. Without conscious thought, he left his car on the side street and trudged toward the wide oak tree where he and Jillian had ministered to the teens.

A dreamlike stupor encompassed him. He neared the exact spot where he'd prayed with the boy to ask Jesus into his life.

What? Was he going to speak to teens now about God's work in his life? Far from it. He had no more strength. Couldn't live like God wanted him to. Exhaustion overcame him. He'd become one big failure.

Let us not be weary in well doing: for in due season we shall reap, if we faint not.

Riley flinched. That thought wasn't for him. Maybe for some other Christian, like Tim or Pastor Taylor. Not him. He'd botched his life.

The path took him farther into the park. As he'd expected, a couple of kids loitered under an elm, handing some dealer their hard-earned cash. The man with long curly hair jerked his head to each side, then passed the boys a small bag.

Done. The two kids might as well give up now. Their lives would never be the same. Riley knew.

Riley crept a little closer, his pulse pounding, suspicion running rampant. The dealer's face became visible.

James.

Bleak despair overwhelmed Riley. He was doing nothing to prevent the deal from going down. His words were empty threats. Like his life.

The two teen boys drifted toward the commons, and James jammed the cash into his pocket. Riley watched it all, still floundering in his surreal world as he inched closer. What did it matter now? God had given up on him.

James looked up at Riley. His eyes widened, and his mouth dropped open.

"How ya doing?" He gave a sardonic laugh. "Looks like you're busy at work."

"Uh…yeah." His old cell-mate balled his fists in front of his chest like he expected a confrontation. "And it looks like you got yourself in a little trouble. All that blood on your face and shirt."

No need to go into the details. "Naw. Just a bloody nose." Bile filled his throat. Cold sweat broke out along his neck and under his arms. He had to do this. "What are you selling, dude?"

The other man dropped his fisted hands to his sides.

"Look. I gotta make a living. Get out of here, you and your high and mighty religion."

Riley swallowed hard. His heart sank. His rent, tuition, the cost of living in Washington. He couldn't afford it on a janitor's income. How could he have been so stupid? "Naw. I was thinking about taking you up on your job offer."

The dealer's mouth fell open again. "I...I don't know if I trust you. Are you serious?"

Riley's words came from someone else, not him. "Yeah, I'm serious."

James puffed out his chest and took a step closer. "Hey, man. I told you before, if you want the big money, hang with me." He lowered his voice to a hoarse whisper. "I don't have to remind you, kids are gonna get it from somewhere. It's everywhere. You know that. Why not make the bucks?"

A cold wave of shame inched down Riley's spine and made him shiver. *I'm a loser, so what does it matter?*

James stepped back, his eyes narrowed to slits. He lifted his palms. "Hey, you're not working for the cops?"

An evil snicker spewed out of Riley's throat. "Me, are you kidding?"

"Look. Let's sit on this for a few days." James pushed a small plastic bag of the white powder in Riley's hand. "Try this, for old time's sake, and get back to me." He snaked through the trees toward the street.

Riley forced himself to look at the bag of coke. *Okay, are you happy now? Back to the old life.* He shoved the packet in his jean's pocket and turned toward his car.

After a few steps he came to a standstill. A vision of Jillian, her radiant eyes, filled his mind. Her love for God. The clinic for girls. Her sense of responsibility.

Riley had wanted, no, prayed for her to receive the Lord's forgiveness. Every day. To comprehend that Jesus had paid for her wrongs—what she'd done ten years ago. By His death on the cross, she'd been forgiven and made new.

As if a hand slapped him across the face, the truth dawned. What about him? How could he want these things for Jillian if he didn't allow them for himself?

He hesitated a few feet from his car. A verse from Pastor Taylor's sermon last week burned in his memory. "No temptation has seized you except what is common to man."

Joy surged through his chest. He wasn't the only Christian who'd failed. *Christian?* Yeah, he was still a follower of the Lord Jesus Christ.

God is faithful. He will not let you be tempted beyond what you can bear. Enticement beckoned Riley back to his old way of life, to give up his walk with the Lord.

A breathtaking thought sent a chill up his legs to his arms. Thinking about Jillian, a person he'd harmed years ago, had set him on the right road today. How typical of God. To use all things in our lives for good.

Riley opened his mouth and let the fresh words pour out. "But when you are tempted, he will also provide a way out so that you can stand up under it." *What way?* Riley glanced up, looking straight ahead at the little church across the street. The marquee said, "For we do not have a high priest who is unable to sympathize with our weaknesses."

Wow, Lord. I think I get the message. You understand my pain because You went through so much hurt for me. You died on a cross to save me from my sins. From my drug use and dealing and the shortcuts.

How could I turn my back on Him? Jesus had made an enormous sacrifice.

Hope consumed his spirit. He hadn't used since he'd been set free by the Lord, so why should he now. He swerved back toward the park in the opposite direction from the commons.

The path led to the waterfalls that fed the Chako Chee Creek, where a cascade flowed onto a couple of large boulders before plunging down into the stream. Riley waded into the cold water, clothes and all. What did it matter about his garments? They were covered with blood. He could wash them at the same time God renewed him.

Tromping through the knee-deep icy creek, his feet wobbled on the rocky bottom. He gained his balance, opened the bag of white powder, and sprinkled it over the water. Coke floated on top where it danced and bubbled on the surface. Then a little whirlpool sucked it under.

Melting snow from the Cascade Mountains filled the rushing stream. His legs were numb, yet warmth caressed them and circled through his body.

Riley climbed up on one of the boulders and moved so the water's flow could gush over him. He lifted his arms up and tilted his head back, allowing the flow to run over his face.

God hadn't turned His back on him, though he'd turned his back on God for a moment. The water was a symbol of the spring of living water that had cleansed him while he was in jail. The precious flow continued to wash him. He'd never thirst again. This stream of water wouldn't run dry.

A jubilant laugh gurgled from his throat. He crawled down from the rock and waded out of the stream, his hair and clothes dripping on the path. God had rescued him from a miry pit. No matter what turn his life took, the Lord wouldn't forsake him, working all things for good.

Only moments before, he'd allowed discouragement to control him instead of the Holy Spirit. But now he was sure. With every daybreak, God would be by his side making His mercies new each day.

Two teens on skateboards scooting along the path gawked at Riley and howled. They stepped off the boards and pointed at him. One poked the other in the ribs.

Riley didn't care. God's healing power filled him. His clothes clung to his body, but he continued on to his car. So what if the seats got wet. They'd dry.

A plan formulated in his mind. He pulled out from his parking place, knowing exactly what he would do, confess to Tim that he'd almost slipped back into the old lifestyle.

When he found a space in front of the church, he got out of the car and jogged through the front door and down the corridor to Tim's office.

The counselor sat at his desk writing something on a pad of paper. He looked up, eyes wide. "What happened, dude? Did you get caught in the sprinkler or something?"

Riley ran a hand through his wet hair, a bit chilled from the cold water despite the warm July weather.

"Hey, man. You got a minute? I'd like to talk."

"Uh…yeah. Sit down." Tim bounded to his feet. "Wait. Don't sit down yet." He grabbed an old towel from a closet near his desk and spread it on the cloth-covered chair. "Okay, now."

Tim covered his mouth, stifling a snicker. "To tell you the truth, I've never had a wet client before. I have a feeling you've got a story for me."

At first the words stuck in Riley's throat. He'd told Tim about a lifetime of mistakes and God's faithfulness, but how could he tell him he'd almost fallen into temptation?

After he cleared his throat, the words poured, interrupted only by Riley's attempts to swallow down his emotions. But he didn't care. Tim had probably seen guys cry before.

When Riley described his swimming excursion in Chako Chee Creek, Tim smiled. "Chako Chee. Did you know those are the Chinook words for *to become new*?"

"To become new. That's appropriate, I'd say."

Tim nodded. "I've got to tell you, you had me forcing tears back a couple of times. You know, you reminded me of the time before Roxanne and I married. I struggled with some major obstacles in my life. Mostly anger. I almost got fired from my job as a youth pastor."

The guy's words blew Riley away. Tim? He'd always thought the counselor had it all together.

His friend scooted his chair closer to Riley. "As you told your story, I couldn't help but think of the magnificent words of our Lord's Prayer. '*Give us this day* our daily bread.' He desires to supply all your needs and He will. 'Forgive us our debts *as we forgive* our debtors.' Something God required of Roxanne and me, to forgive others and ourselves. In your case—forgiving yourself. He's delivered you from your past just as God tells us to ask him to *deliver us* from evil.

Tim stroked his chin. "But enough of my preaching. Look, the janitor we had is leaving. I need to check with the elders, but I'm pretty sure I can offer you the job."

Riley rose from the chair, not dripping as much as before. "I think I'd better start by mopping up your office."

~

An idea began to take shape in Riley's mind. He stepped to his car and poked his head in, retrieving his cell phone from the glove box. Good thing he hadn't taken it with him to the park. Walking around to the back of the church, he hiked down the woodland trail. When he arrived at the break in the fence, he peered around for something to serve his purpose, the plan still forming in his brain.

The memory of the beautiful doctor who possessed his heart floated into his thoughts. He might never have a relationship with her again, but he prayed she'd forgive him. For her sake. Hadn't Tim talked about forgiveness?

Riley loved Jillian, but she'd found someone else. She didn't feel the same way as he did about her, yet he still wanted to pray for her, encourage her and lift her up in the Lord. She'd been through so much. Suffered because of his mistakes as well as her own.

Pure joy bubbled up from his heart. Near the old

stone wall, a flat rock about the size of a frying pan lid lay on the ground. *Yes, that's what I'll do.*

He pulled his cell out of his dry shirt pocket. If he called her now, she wouldn't answer because she was working her clinic hours. He could leave a message.

His pulse leaped when he heard her voice. "Hello. This is Dr. Coleman. I can't take a call right now, but press one to leave me a message, and I'll get back to you. If this is an emergency, call 911."

Riley cleared his throat and waited for the signal. "Jillian, this is Riley. Please don't hang up. I'm calling now because I know you don't want to talk to me. And I don't blame you. Please, just listen."

Leaning against the wall, he cleared his croaky throat and tried not to sound like an idiot. "I don't expect you to forgive me and if you did, I'd never allow myself to dream…"

He'd almost said dream about a life with her. "I just want to encourage you. Look, you never have to talk to me again. Walk the other way if you see me at church. I understand. Still I want to bring you the same kind of hope God has given me."

With his hand on his forehead, he continued. "I'm going to write you a note every Sunday and Wednesday and place it under the gray and rose-colored rock out on the woodland trail." Riley knelt and ran his fingers over the smooth stone. "You know the place, on the south side of the rock wall at the opening. Remember…" Riley remembered. The day he held Jillian in his arms here. She'd cried and told him about the abortion.

"I promise I'll never be there when you are." He placed his palm over his heart. "I'll stick the notes under the rock early in the morning so you'll never run into me. I promise, Jillian." He drew his hand through his hair and paced along the forest floor. "Just allow me the privilege of encouraging you. I'll always pray for you."

~

Jillian shook Tim Garrett's hand and smiled at him. "Thank you for the message today. I think this is the first time I've heard you preach."

"I don't get a chance at the pulpit very often." Tim grinned at her. "I'm glad the elders suggested I fill in while Pastor Taylor's on vacation."

"Thank you for those words today about forgiveness. They touched me."

"I'm glad. God taught me those lessons as well."

Jillian turned right and walked down the sidewalk around the church that led to the woodland trail out back. Riley had said Sundays and Wednesdays, so the first note should be there.

At first, she'd tried to ignore his phone message. The notes could blow away, for all she cared. But then, what would it hurt to pick up one? She didn't have to read any others.

Colorful flowers grew in the beds near the back lawn. Someone made an effort to see the grounds looked well cared for. The familiar path appeared ahead.

A warm breeze caressed her skin as she continued down the trail. On either side, tall Douglas firs lined the path. The route led to a cleared area where grass, ferns, and wild flowers grew in abundance. Maybe a homesteader from another century had lived there once with his family. The well-worn path meandered through the break in the old stone fence.

The rock by the wall near the opening became visible. Jillian slowed her pace. A colorful piece of granite lay on the ground. She knelt and picked up the edge. Her heart raced. A plastic bag, the kind that zipped up, lay on the soil under the rock, a piece of white paper visible inside.

She unzipped the bag, pulling out a neatly creased piece of plain white paper. A masculine scrawl filled half of the sheet.

Dear Jillian. As long as I live, I'll always regret what I did. How I took advantage of a beautiful and innocent young college girl. I pray you find it in your heart to forgive me. You don't have to tell me. Only tell the Lord. But let me get on with my purpose today—to bring you hope from God's word. First of all, God has forgiven you for everything in your life you ever did that wasn't in His will. In fact, he doesn't even remember the past any longer. Hebrews says, "I will remember their sins no more." God has forgiven both of us, Jillian. Take encouragement in that. Until next time. In Christ, Riley.

Jillian refolded the note and carefully tucked it in her pocket. His words did encourage her. She was grateful. Maybe she'd come back on Wednesday and read the next note. But one thing she knew for sure. She'd never allow herself to trust him again.

Chapter Twenty

Riley parked two blocks from the park and sidled out. *Good.* Unwanted observers wouldn't spot him here. With a swipe over his damp brow, he pinned his sunglasses on his ears. Dark jeans and a black tee shirt should serve his purpose.

Blood pounded in his temples, but with extra effort, he regulated his steps, keeping each at a fixed pace. He couldn't afford to appear anxious.

The park and the commons nestled within the clearing came into sight. James would be close by, hidden somewhere between some of the thick bushes and trees. The sun sank a bit lower in the western horizon. He expected the drug dealer to infiltrate the area this time of day.

From a glance over his shoulder, he could see no one followed him, that he could tell. Blowing his breath out in one steady stream, he identified his former cellmate, half of him anyway. His back was toward Riley, partially hidden by a tree trunk. No customers nearby at the moment.

With a few faltering steps, Riley crept unnoticed as yet toward the steely drug dealer, stepping around the blackberry bush to approach him from the other side.

A rip and a tug on his shirt caught his attention. "Oh, man." He wrangled the cloth away from the bush as his forehead broke out in a sweat.

His old cellmate jerked toward him with a frown. So much for remaining incognito. James' chin drooped, and he opened his mouth.

Riley willed his voice to remain calm. "Hey, man. You look like you didn't believe I'd come back."

James pressed his lips into a bundle. "What do you want?"

"Nothing." Riley swallowed a gulp he hoped James wouldn't notice. "I'm just stopping by for a chat."

"Yeah, right." James shifted from one foot to another.

"How's business?" Riley stuffed his hands in his pockets, glad James couldn't hear the pounding of his heart.

The other man scratched his head. "Last time we talked, you said you wanted to join the organization." He cocked an eyebrow. "How'd you like the stuff I gave you?"

With sweaty palms, Riley tried to act cool, though a clan of hyenas romped through his stomach. "Yeah, fine."

James took a step toward him. "Well, what did you decide? You still looking for work?"

"Maybe." Riley didn't like lying, but he had a purpose to accomplish.

A slow smile formed on James' face. "Well, this is the second time you've approached me. I'd say you've come to your senses. Look, I've got some decent rock today." He glanced to his right, then to his left. He stuffed a hand in his hoodie and pulled out two bags of the irregularly shaped crystals. "Take one for yourself. And if you can sell the other in the next thirty minutes, I might consider you." He held both out to Riley.

The rush of the two undercover cops startled Riley at first, though he expected them. The first guy, a backwards Mariner's cap sitting on his head, held a pistol to James' ribs.

"What the..." James wrenched away but the second cop, equipped with bulging muscles, wrestled his hands behind him and snapped cuffs on. "You're under arrest." The muscle man read James the Miranda rights.

He uttered a curse word that in Riley's earlier days wouldn't have scorched his ears. Today, though, the filth lay like trash strewn on the ground by the man who had no thoughts of anyone but himself. "I knew you were working for the cops." He spit on the grass. "Hey, this guy set me up."

The man with the Mariner's cap, whom Riley recognized as Tony, clutched James' arm. "No setup here. You approached Mr. Mathis. We've been watching your activity for weeks now. And his, too." Tony aimed a thumb over his shoulder in Riley's direction. "He's been dealing something too, but it's not drugs."

"Hey, he asked me for it. Said he wanted to sell." James hissed.

"You have no proof of that. The stuff is in your possession, not his." Tony tightened his hold on James while muscle man frisked him retrieving the rest of the bags of rock and placing them in a plastic container. "Mr. Mathis, did you intend to sell that substance to someone?"

"No." It felt good to know he really meant that *no*.

"Hey, you piece of..." James jerked toward Riley.

"Let's go." Tony and the muscle guy, on either side of James, marched him toward the street.

Riley caught up with them. "Do you need anything else from me?"

"No, not for now. But we'll be in touch. Thanks, dude. You did the right thing, telling us about your near misstep with the drugs you got from this dealer. But you didn't commit a crime that day because you paid nothing, didn't use, and aren't in possession now. Your cooperation has led us to another one of these lowlife dealers. We spotted him a couple of months ago but hadn't caught him in action. The city of Woodlyn thanks you. We thank you."

Riley wiped away the sweat that had already begun to drip down under his sunglasses. One of the best decisions he'd ever made was to go to the cops and confess, telling them about the day he accepted the coke from James. Though he'd taken a chance on getting locked up again, it had been worth it.

It was kind of exciting, working with the law. Riley puffed out his chest and brushed his hands off. James wouldn't be selling drugs to kids for quite a while. A third offense should keep him in prison for a long time.

~

With a tug on the pull cord, Jillian lifted the mauve mini-blinds on the double paned window. The hot tub and the adults' pool beckoned from the ground level, but the notes held her captive. She padded back to the couch, sank down into the thickly woven fabric, and glimpsed the stack of papers, Riley's letters in a neat pile on her walnut coffee table.

After all these weeks, he'd kept his word. He never made an appearance when she took the trail out to the rock wall every Wednesday and Sunday.

Each time her heart had pounded a little harder when she retrieved the plastic bag and a handwritten note. At first she didn't want to acknowledge what her heart told her, but gradually, she knew.

The letter on top she'd found only this morning after church. With her feet propped on the coffee table and her head resting on the couch pillow, she lifted the paper to eye level and read again.

"He stilled the storm to a whisper: the waves of the sea were hushed. He guided them to their desired haven." Jillian, those words from Psalms are a promise. Whatever direction your life takes, God is there to guide and direct you. If He put the clinic for pregnant girls on your heart, it will come to pass.

Dear God in Heaven, allow Jillian to see Your hand each day as she walks through this life and serves you. In Christ, Riley.

Holding the note over her heart, she drew in a satisfying breath. God didn't leave her like an orphan in this world to stumble around blindly. He loved her now, but just as amazing, He had loved and accepted her before—before she knew of His forgiveness.

She dropped the letter on the couch and reached for another.

"Jesus replied, what is impossible with men is possible with God." Our Lord put the clinic on your heart and though it seems impossible now, He can make it happen. Believe that it will. Do everything in your power to get it going and trust the Lord for the results.

Lord, I pray for Jillian. She loves you and desires to serve you. Open up the doors for her clinic. In Jesus' name. Riley.

Like a small child overflowing with anticipation of new toys on Christmas morning, hope filled Jillian, hope and confidence. God would accomplish what He placed in her heart.

She lifted her gaze heavenward. Riley believed in her. He had caught her vision, God's vision of the clinic. Though she'd doubted so many times the doors to the Jeremiah House would ever open, the clinic became more real now than ever before.

With another note in her hand, she paced to the window and read aloud.

"And so we know and rely on the love God has for us. God is love. Whoever lives in love lives in God, and God in Him. Jillian, I need you to know how much God loves you. He treasures and values you. Always remember you are His child. Lord, I pray that Jillian will realize how important she is to You. In Jesus name. Riley."

Jesus had forgiven her for killing her child, but she always doubted He could really love her. Riley had reminded her He did. Like a small child whose faithful daddy stayed by her hospital bed all night, she had the same assurance about God.

Once she'd accepted that truth, she had to acknowledge another. Setting the note back on the table with the others, she ambled to the kitchen to make a cup of chamomile tea. As dawn slowly and with certainty brings a new day, she'd begun to understand. Her feelings for Jett were shallow and based solely on attraction. For Riley, she possessed an abiding love, rooted in God and His word.

She treasured his Christian values and adored the way he encouraged her and prayed for her. Even the memory of his boyish face and piercing-blue eyes snatched her breath away.

The whistling of the kettle she'd filled with water brought her back from her reflections. Pouring the bubbling liquid over the tea bag produced a pleasant aroma, like apples. It made her envision a restful Sunday afternoon with Riley, so different than her weekends with Jett. He'd always wanted to sightsee, water ski, or go sailing in the Sound.

Jett. As if she'd swallowed sour milk, her stomach clinched. She had to come to terms with the truth she became more aware of in light of her love for Riley. Whether he was in her life or not, she couldn't commit to a marriage with the doctor. She didn't love him enough. She didn't love him at all.

Like her father, Jett was all about work. No room for anything less than perfection. She'd never live up to his standards.

The timer beeped, and she tossed the tea bag in the garbage. Mug in hand, she meandered back to the large windows. Though she might hurt or disappoint Jett, that would be better than a loveless marriage for both of them. She needed to tell him as soon as possible.

She picked up her cell from the coffee table and pushed Jett's speed dial number.

"Hey, beautiful. I was thinking about calling you. We still need to clear up that little misunderstanding we had in front of the hospital a few weeks ago. I've been giving you some space, in case you were worried. Since I don't anticipate any deliveries this afternoon, how about we drive up to Stephen's Pass?"

The times at the hospital when Jett had looked through her like she was invisible, she hadn't cared, but now, the way he took over the conversation before she even told him why she'd called bothered her. "Could you come to my apartment right away?"

~

The doorbell dinged. Jillian pushed her nerves aside and threw her shoulders back. Even though her heart pounded at the thought of the task ahead, she found courage and marched to the door. No more putting this off.

Jett had asked her to marry him, even bought her a ring. He loved her in his own way, and she didn't want to hurt him. *Lord, allow me to speak my words with kindness and grace.*

When she opened the door, he waltzed in wearing a colossal smile on his face. Closing the door behind him, he pulled her into his arms and pressed his lips on hers. "I knew you'd come to your senses sooner or later." He patted his pocket. "I still have your ring, right here." A smile lifted the corners of his mouth, and he grabbed her left hand.

Every muscle in her body stiffened. This wouldn't be easy. She jerked her hand away. "Please sit down. We need to talk."

"Hey, sweetheart, this day is too beautiful for such a long face. What's up?" Jett smiled down at her, not taking her suggestion to take a seat.

"I need to tell you how much I respect your ability as a doctor and a medical professional." Jillian fought tears of regret that the man who stood in front of her may not have given his life to the Lord. For a short while, he'd feel hurt and rejection. But she hoped he wouldn't become bitter and turn against his Creator.

"Well, thanks, Jillian. You're pretty competent as well. Now if you'd just get over that notion of working for free in some clinic for girls who couldn't figure out how to protect themselves..."

Her fingers curled into fists at her side. "Let me finish. I respect you as a professional but that's where it ends." Her voice wobbled. "I don't want to hurt you. You're a great guy with a fine future, but I can't share it with you." She studied her shoes. "I'm sorry I waited so long to tell you."

"I was right. It's the janitor, isn't it? You've got a thing for him." Jett's brow furrowed. His fair complexion darkened to an ugly red. "How can you fall for a lowlife like him? He'll never be able to support you, much less give you the kind of life you're used to."

Support her? Riley supported her in a way Jett never could. He encouraged her with scriptures and believed in her dreams.

"And something else. I did a little poking around. You want to know what I found out? He's a felon. Just got out of jail." Jett picked up her hand again. "Jillian, I don't want you to have anything to do with him anymore. He's not a safe person to associate with."

The irony of Jett's statement sent prickles down her arms. Years ago Riley was different, but God had changed him. She felt more comfortable around Riley than she did Jett. She never knew when he'd mock her.

"I'm aware of Riley's past. But so you know, we don't talk anymore. This doesn't have anything to do with him. I'm very sorry, but I don't think it would work with us." She touched his arm. "Can't we be friends for now?"

"I couldn't be friends with someone who makes such ridiculously poor choices." Jett shrugged her hand off. "You're an educated doctor, for Pete's sake. And yet you're thinking like an empty-headed schoolgirl. When you come to your senses, give me a call. Maybe I'll let you come crawling back." He yanked open the door and stormed out.

She hated the ugliness of the scene but couldn't help the feeling of relief that followed. Marrying Jett would have been a huge mistake. How could she have been so blind? Riley wanted only to encourage her in the Lord, with nothing in it for him. Jett was a pompous, arrogant, selfish...

The pile of notes remained on her coffee table. She needed the support they provided. Later she would make plans to accomplish what her heart, her mind, and now her spirit told her to do.

~

"Hi, it's me. May I come in?" Riley tapped on the door and gave it a push.

"Hi, honey." Mom stuck her head around the kitchen entrance. "Come on in."

Her latest newborn lay in the cradle in the living room. The noisy voices coming from the backyard told him the other kids were out playing. He wandered in toward the sound of a spoon tapping against a pan.

His mother stood at the stove stirring something in a pot that smelled like chicken stew.

Dexter looked up from his newspaper.

"You're just in time for Sunday dinner." She gave him a quick hug and turned away to pull fresh baked rolls from the oven.

"Oh, I don't plan to stay long, thank you." Riley fingered the keys in his pocket and cleared his throat. "I need to talk to you and Dex for a minute."

Mom sank into one of the kitchen chairs. "Anything wrong, honey?"

Dex cleared his throat. "Look, Riley, I may have been too quick to fire you a few weeks ago." His stepfather gave him a wary look and folded his newspaper.

"No, Dexter. I don't blame you. The good news is I've got another job at my church. But I would like to help you with the books at Woodlyn Maintenance sometime if you ever come to trust me. I mean, when I've finished a few more business classes."

"I uh…We'll see." Dexter ran a hand through his hair.

Riley chuckled under his breath. He still hadn't gained Dexter's full confidence. But God was his provider, not Woodlyn Maintenance. "I came here for a couple of reasons. I wanted to tell you about my plan. The community college counted some of the courses I took while I was in prison, credits that will transfer easily enough to the university. The registrar's office also gave me credit for the two classes I finished before I went to jail. If I put my mind to it, I'll be able to have my degree in three years and be a full-fledged accountant."

"That's wonderful. I know you can do it." Mom squeezed his arm.

"Thanks, Mom. But that's not the main reason for my visit." He'd put this off for too long and today was his chance. He glanced at Dexter then to Mom. "First I want to ask your forgiveness. I've caused both of you a lot of heartache through the years."

Dexter's eyes widened as if weighing Riley's words.

Mom dabbed at her eyes with a tissue and sniffed.

"I'm confident with God's help, my life is on a different course now, and I intend to make you both proud of me, one day."

"Riley, I'm proud of you now." Mom stood to give him a hug. "I love you, son."

"And I'm proud of you, too." Dexter gave Riley a punch on his shoulder. "I've seen you grow from the boy who went to prison to the ex-con stuck in the *shortcut mode*, to the man you are now, someone who wants to do the right thing because it's the right thing to do. A man who turned his life around."

"Thanks. But you've got one thing wrong. It wasn't me who turned my life around. It was God."

Chapter Twenty-One

Uh, oh. Twenty minutes late. Jillian didn't mean for that to happen, especially this morning. Her brakes squealed as she whipped into a parking place at the end of the lot. At least she'd make the last few minutes of worship.

She yanked her key out of the ignition and grasped the door handle, her mission fully formed in her mind.

Forgive yourself even as I have forgiven you.

Her hand flew to her throat. She'd heard the words as clearly as if Someone had spoken them aloud.

She leaned back, the headrest supporting her. Only this morning she'd read in Matthew the story of the unforgiving debtor. Jesus ended the story by saying we need to pardon our brothers from our hearts.

Through the years she'd learned not to hold grudges against others. In the last month she'd made the conscious decision to even forgive her father knowing that he only had her best interests at heart.

But what about her? If God could demonstrate His grace, and He commanded her to do the same for others, she needed to apply it to herself as well. Like a splash of cool water in her face on a summer day, she understood. She'd disobeyed God by not forgiving herself. But that was about to change. She could walk forward without the restrictive guilt now.

With a joyful squeal, Jillian stepped out of the car. She took a breath of the perfumed air on the glorious Sunday morning.

The double doors led into the empty foyer. "Beautiful Things" wafted from the sanctuary. The words encouraged her. God had made something beautiful from her life. How dare she deny it by saying one of God's children wasn't excused for wrong doings? *Thank you, Lord for bringing me to this place in my heart and this place of worship.*

With a few unsteady steps, she crept up the center aisle. About half way on her right, Riley stood, his hand raised in praise.

Her pulse tapping a persistent rhythm, she took cautious steps down the aisle, like a teen trying to sneak home two hours late. The rows of worshipers, some with closed eyes and arms lifted, seemed oblivious to her as she passed.

Jillian savored the airy sensation in her chest. Now more positive than ever of her decision, a grin spread her lips.

But what about Riley? How would he respond?

He still hadn't noticed her when she squeezed in next to him, accidentally bumping his shoulder.

He opened his eyes wide and gaped at her. "Hello," he whispered.

"Can I sit by you?" She moved her lips without making a sound.

The same flabbergasted expression remained on his face as he nodded.

When the congregation sat, Jillian tried relaxing

into the pew cushions, but her stomach insisted on doing somersaults. What if Riley told her to get lost? Or if he'd found somebody else?

After the worship team laid their instruments down in back and left the stage, Pastor Taylor rose to his platform. "Beloved, this is the day the Lord has made. Let us rejoice and be glad in it."

"Amen." Voices rang in unison.

The bulletin from last week poked out from the center of Jillian's Bible. The blank space on the back would be enough room. She pulled a pen out of her purse and scribbled. *Could we talk? After the service out on the trail?* She placed the note in Riley's open Bible.

He gave her a quick look, picked up the paper, and glanced at it.

How would he react to her suggestion? Jillian's chest tightened.

Dropping the bulletin on his Bible, he turned to her again, lifted a brow, and slowly gave her a half-grin. Then he nodded.

Heat filled her cheeks. Oh, she was worse than a teenager with a crush. Jillian distracted Riley from Pastor Taylor's message.

With a glance toward the clock on the sidewall, she cringed. The service was almost over. She hadn't heard a word the pastor said.

"And we know that in all things God works for the good of those who love Him, who have been called according to His purpose. My brethren, I'd like to encourage you today. Are problems dragging you down, overwhelming you? Be encouraged by God's word. Though you may not see a way out right now, know that God is and will turn all these things around and use them for His glory." Their pastor raised his hand to the congregation. "Go in His love as you serve Him."

~

The lump in Jillian's stomach threatened to turn into rock. Though Riley ambled beside her along the trail, what would he say when he discovered her reason for bringing him to the note drop?

The evergreen scent and the cool breeze brought a measure of courage. Not far now. Only a short distance and they'd arrive at the spot where she'd visited for the last four weeks.

The now familiar wall and the flat gray and rose-colored rock came into view. She stopped in front of the stone, picked it up, and pulled out the plastic bag. Riley must've left it there earlier this morning like he'd done every Wednesday and Sunday. She placed another plastic bag with her note underneath and dropped the rock back to the ground.

"It's for you."

With a raised eyebrow, he gave her a puzzled look. "For me?" He scratched his neck under his white dress shirt but stood motionless before her.

She raised her hands to her hips. Maybe he wanted to act stubborn or tease her. Yet that didn't seem like the guy she knew. "Just read it, Riley." She held her breath waiting to see his next move.

He knelt down, raised the rock, and grasped the plastic bag. Staring at the note, he stood and drew in a long breath. With trembling hands, he pulled the paper out, unfolded the letter, and flipped it open. A frown furrowed his brow.

Her whispered plea formed the words. "Read it out loud." He seemed so hesitant, she feared he might take one look, toss it to the ground, and walk away. Maybe he'd finally lost patience with her, especially after the way she'd avoided him these last weeks.

Fingers rubbing his chin, he glanced at her and back at the note. He read. "Riley, I can't wait any longer to tell you. I'm so sorry about how I've behaved, especially during the last weeks. I was wrong." After one more glance at her, he began again. "Christ forgave me for my mistakes when He saved me. He commanded us to do the same. I've forgiven you, Riley, and myself. And I need to ask your pardon as well. In a way, that night I used you for my own need, too. I'm sorry."

Riley shot her a look, his mouth open and eyes wide, as if he found her words unbelievable.

"I love you with all my heart. I only pray you feel the same about me. In Christ, Jillian."

The note floated from his fingers to settle by his feet. He cleared his throat and slid his hands onto her shoulders. "I stand here amazed. I don't know what to say, Jillian."

She looked up into his eyes when he drew her into his arms, no words needed. She'd come home. She and Riley had a future together. God had opened the doors.

"Jillian?" Riley stiffened and dropped his hands. "I can't believe you chose me instead of my competition, the doctor."

She traced a finger down his cheek, amused he'd think of Jett as competition. Though she no longer saw him as a candidate for a marriage partner, Riley probably thought so. "I told him I didn't want to continue our relationship. He's not the godly man who stole my heart."

Cupping her hand, she smoothed her palm along the rough stubble of Riley's chin. She'd missed him. In slow motion, she leaned in and brushed her lips over his. A bit bold, but she didn't care. Her heart ruled. She explored the soft skin of his mouth, coaxing him to kiss her back.

After a long moment, Riley stepped away and studied her face, a half smile playing at the corners of his mouth. He cradled her face with both hands before his lips took control of hers.

Jillian lost all sense of time, aware only of her pounding heart and Riley's intoxicating nearness. The trail of warmth his fingers left as they glided over her neck and down her back left her breathless.

His kiss became more urgent. The pressure of his body against hers left her dizzy. Almost out of breath, she whispered. "I'm sorry. I wasn't polite enough to ask you if it was okay, like the first time you kissed me."

His quiet chuckle flooded her with a warm sensation. "Are you kidding? I kissed you back just now in case you hadn't noticed, something I hope to do for a long time to come." He captured her hand and pressed a kiss in her palm. "Jillian, I love you, too. I want to spend the rest of my life with you."

"I feel the same way…" She ran two fingers across her lips and touched his mouth.

Lines wrinkled his forehead, and he grasped her arm. "Can we…can we put the past behind us? Our child?"

A shaft of sunlight shot through the barrier of trees.

At last—to truly experience forgiveness for herself and Riley was a miracle. She basked in the reality. "Our baby is in heaven. We'll see her or him again someday. In the meantime, I'm hoping we'll be blessed with children in this life." She lowered her lashes.

"I think the first time I fell in love with you was when God allowed me to see your heart and His call on your life to minister to young girls who made unwise choices." He drew her hands to his chest. "Remember the verse Pastor cited today. How God uses all things for our good. That counts for even the messes we've made in the past."

A tear glided down her cheek. "You'll never know how much your words bless me."

With his thumb, he wiped away the moisture. He drew her into his arms and tightened his hold.

A buzzing in her pocket tickled her leg. "Oh. I forgot. I'm on call." She pulled her smart phone out and lifted it to her ear. "Yes, this is Dr. Coleman."

"Hello, doctor. This is Mrs. Duncan. Just to let you know, both Mrs. Garrett and Mrs. Colton have been admitted."

"All right. I'm on my way." Jillian smiled and shoved her cell back in her jeans. "I've got to go to the hospital for a delivery. Make that two deliveries. Holly Colton and Roxanne Garrett are both in labor."

JUNE FOSTER

Chapter Twenty-Two

Riley mustered every bit of courage he could find. Proposing to a woman wasn't an everyday occurrence, especially a woman like Dr. Jillian Coleman. Had God brought him far enough to be able to take responsibility for a wife and a home?

With a tap on his shoulder, Jillian grinned. "Riley Mathis. What's going on? Tim didn't send us out on mission work today." After another glance, she wrinkled her nose. "It's not polite to keep secrets."

As if Jillian would escape, he grasped her hand tighter. The path leading to the falls meandered through tall Douglas firs. Fresh air filled his lungs. If he never parted from this woman again, he'd be happy.

A wide smile stretched across his face, a permanent fixture today. Nothing stood between them any longer.

First, he heard the splatter of water as it splashed on the round rocks at the Chako Chee falls. After a few more steps down the path, he spotted the stream where he'd waded the day he'd felt so low—the day of his baptism. It made the perfect spot to ask Jillian to be his wife.

"I don't think we're going to minister to teens again today." Jillian grinned and tugged on his hand. "Why won't you tell me what's going on?"

Jillian's gentle teasing sent a wallop to his stomach. She knew why he'd brought her here. "It's time we thought about us."

The clearing where the waterfall pooled into the creek emerged ahead. He pointed to the park bench across the path, so close to the flow the spray would probably mist them. "Let's sit here." He pulled her alongside him and motioned her to sit.

The absence of people jogging and walking along the trail brought him a measure of relief. He didn't exactly need an audience for this. Riley covered her hand with his. With his other, his fingers traced the outline of the small box in his pocket. "I thank the Lord for bringing us together. I'm still amazed how God turned our mistakes into good and sent you back to me."

"We're not the same people we were then. We're wiser, stronger. That's the best part."

"Thank God. Only He could accomplish something like that." He squeezed her hand and tried to ignore the inferno rising up his neck. "Jillian, I want more for us. I have a very important question to ask you. I think you can guess what it is."

Her lips parted in a smile. "I think I can."

Elation surged in Riley like the bubbling waters that leapt and danced in the Chako Chee. "I want to make it clear to you, first, that I intend to continue proving to you, Mom and Dexter, and my church family that I can take responsibility for my life. I want to take care of you and provide for you and any family God chooses to bless us with." Riley released Jillian's hand and laced his fingers.

"I was waiting to tell you, but I received a grant from the Charles W. Colson Scholarship fund. It will pay for my tuition and books. Dexter wants me to do the accounting for Woodlyn Maintenance, and I intend to keep working at the church."

"I'm so proud of you." Jillian threw her arms around him in a fierce hug.

Riley knelt down on one knee on the grass in front of her and pulled out the ring box, grateful his mom had made the offer.

He took the diamond set in a white gold band out of the box. "This ring is the one my father gave my mother before they were married." His voice quivered. "It means a lot to me. I hope you'll accept it."

Jillian gasped. "Oh, Riley, that makes it even more precious. I don't know what to say."

"Say you'll marry me."

Her eyes shown bright with unshed tears. "I'd love to."

The ring slipped easily over her finger, and he snuggled next to her on the park bench.

Jillian cuddled closer, the diamond on her finger. If he said it a hundred times, it probably still wouldn't sink in. Three magical words revolved in his head. She'd said yes.

Riley folded his arms around her. His lips traveled from the tender skin of her neck to her bare shoulder. His pounding pulse persuaded him he'd better suggest a short engagement. After all, they'd waited ten years to get it right.

As he stopped to think about the effect she had on him, more heat crept into his cheeks. "I forgot for a moment we're in a public park. I'm sorry." Good thing the path was deserted.

"You're right. But one of these days, we'll be married… and in private."

He groaned his answer. "I can't wait."

~

Jillian drummed her fingers on her kitchen counter, barely able to contain her excitement. Would Mom ever pick up the phone?

"Hello, honey. I'm so glad to hear from you." Mom's sweet voice rushed over her like a Beethoven concerto. "I'm going to keep reminding you about your promise to visit next winter."

Jillian giggled. "Don't worry, Mom. I'll be there, but I'll probably bring a friend."

"A friend? Is she someone you work with?"

"Well, in a way." Jillian snickered. "But she's a *he*."

"Oh, okay, dear. We do have two guest bedrooms."

Jillian gave a devious laugh. "No need for two bedrooms. We'll be staying in the same one. He'll be my husband by then."

Mom squealed. "Oh, honey. Who...when, where...?" She caught her breath. "Oh, I don't know what I'm saying."

"Sorry, dear. I had to tease you. I'm calling to ask if you could fly out for a week and help me make wedding plans." Joy swelled inside Jillian. "I'll tell you all about it when you get here. And of course, I'll need both you and Dad at the wedding when the time comes." How much easier it was to say the word *Dad* now. God had truly healed her heart.

"You know I'll be there. You've made me the

happiest mom in the world. I love you, honey."

~

The familiar path behind the church took Riley down the woodland trail. Two more weeks. He picked up his pace. Could he wait that long for Jillian Coleman to become Jillian Mathis, his wife?

He loved her so much. The thought of spending his life with the lovely doctor sent a hurricane through him.

When Riley neared the rock wall, he glanced down at the gray and rose stone, his and Jillian's mailbox for the last few months. The sound of crunching leaves and rapid footsteps caught his attention. Another jogger approached him, heading toward the church. As the person neared, Riley finally made out the man's features.

Tim Garrett. Riley hadn't seen him out jogging before, but then, he hadn't jogged near the church either. "Hey, Tim. What are you doing out here?"

Tim lifted his face. The corners of his mouth turned down, and he had dark circles under his eyes. He skidded to a stop, almost tripping over his feet as his shoulders sagged. "Hi, Riley," he mumbled.

"You trying to lose weight or something? You'd better let up a little on this jogging. Looks like it's about to wear you out."

Tim produced a half-way grin. "Naw. It's not the jogging. I'm exercising so maybe I'll be so tired tonight I'll pass out."

"What's the deal? If you don't mind me saying so, you look awful."

"I haven't been getting much sleep." Tim drew a

hand through his hair.

"I'm sorry to hear that." Riley gave him a tap on the shoulder. "Same thing you told me awhile back. If you need somebody to listen, I'm here for you." Surely Tim couldn't be having problems with Roxanne. He'd envisioned them with the perfect marriage.

The low chuckle Tim emitted convinced Riley it couldn't be a marital issue. "It's nothing too serious, but thanks." Tim rubbed his bloodshot eyes. "The baby's been keeping us up. She has her days and nights mixed up. Roxanne's taking a nap right now while our little noisemaker is sleeping."

"So that's what it's like to be a father." Riley slapped his knee as he gave a guffaw. "Maybe I should change my mind about getting married."

Tim's eyes transformed into large circles. "Getting married? You're getting married?"

"Yeah, man." Riley grinned and kicked a rock with his tennis shoe. "I proposed to Jillian and she said yes. Check out the notice on the church bulletin board. We posted one invitation for everyone at Evergreen."

Tim's mouth gaped open. "Way cool. I've been in another world since the baby's birth." He slapped Riley on the shoulder. "Congratulations, dude. I'm happy for both of you."

With one eyebrow raised, Riley gave the counselor a sheepish grin. "Tim?"

"Yeah?"

"I got a question for you."

"Shoot."

"When you paired Jillian and me for the park ministry outreach, was that an inspiration from the Lord or were you playing matchmaker?"

Tim folded his arms over his chest and grinned. "A little of both."

~

A garland of dahlias, mums, and white rosebuds hung over the sanctuary's double doors. Jillian lifted her veil away from her face. In only moments she would walk through those doors and down the aisle. The white satin covered book with guests' signatures and the long-feathered pen rested on a small table with a white lace cloth. Her lovely bridesmaids surrounded her.

The raspberry pink dress fit Holly well. She laughed. "I'm glad you waited until fall to get married, Jillian. I don't think I could've fit into my dress any sooner. The baby fat is just now coming off." She patted her stomach.

Roxy tucked a strand of Jillian's hair back under her veil. "Your bridal up-do is gorgeous, even if I do say so myself. Thank you for giving me the privilege." She smoothed her dress, identical to Holly's, around her slender stomach, all evidence of her pregnancy gone.

"I wouldn't have wanted anyone else to do it, sweetie." Jillian gave her a quick kiss on the cheek.

Jamie floated toward Jillian in her matching pink dress and smiled. She held out a small white Bible. "I believe the only thing you're missing is something borrowed. I'd like you to carry this under your bouquet. It would mean so much to me. The book represents God's transforming power in my life."

Jillian gave her a hug. "Hey, lady, you're going to make me cry and mess up my makeup." She grasped Jamie's hand. "It's a blessing to see your life going in a different direction."

"I can't thank you enough for bringing me to Evergreen. The people in the college group have already become friends." Jamie's eyes glistened, and she patted them with a tissue.

Holly straightened a fold of Jillian's long white gown with its blue satin waist. "Your gorgeous sapphire necklace represents old and blue. So I bet your dress represents new. We've got everything from old to new, borrowed to blue." She giggled.

All Jillian needed. Her heart pounded at the thought of her handsome husband-to-be waiting for her at the altar. Only by God's grace had she and Riley come this far.

~

"You may kiss the bride." Pastor Taylor smiled down on Riley and Jillian.

Riley lost himself in his wife's aquamarine eyes. His gaze drifted down her neck to the necklace resting on her throat's smooth skin. The piece of jewelry delivered a different message than that day at Evergreen when he'd made a fool of himself. Now the woman who wore the stunning sapphire was his wife. He had the right to fix his eyes on her.

Though he couldn't still the wild beating of his heart, Riley lowered his head to Jillian's lips. Anticipation and excitement of their first kiss as husband and wife played tag in his stomach.

A cheer rose from the congregation in the packed sanctuary when Riley finally stepped back. Warmth filled his cheeks.

"Hey, Riley. Only girls blush. What's the deal?" In the front row, Jayke ducked down in his seat and snickered.

With a grin at the kid, Riley shook his head, then gazed into Jillian's lovely face. Holding hands, they turned toward the packed church as husband and wife.

Pastor Taylor's voice rang behind them. "I'd like to introduce Mr. and Mrs. Riley Mathis." Pastor laid his hands on their shoulders. "May God bestow His rich mercies on you as you begin your married life together."

Riley held his wife's hand as they marched down the aisle and into the foyer where he once again drew her into an embrace and kissed her. Tomorrow morning he'd wake up with Jillian by his side and every morning thereafter for all the days God gave them together.

JUNE FOSTER

Epilogue

Three years later

Staring in the mirror and fumbling with his gray and pink tie proved too much for Riley's clumsy fingers. His first day at Glover and Associates Accounting Firm. Without his permission, a herd of cows romped around his nerves. "Jillian, does this tie go okay with my suit?"

His wife, dark circles under her eyes and hair tousled, emerged from the bedroom, carrying a tiny bundle in her arms. "Honey, you're the most handsome guy I know, and it goes perfectly. I picked it out, remember?"

"Oh, yeah." Riley laughed. With a couple of steps, he neared his wife and moved the pink blanket back to peek at his daughter's little face. "Anna, you kept Mom and Dad awake all night. Now it's time for Daddy to go to work, and you're going to snooze all morning in your little bassinette." Even Sam looked sleepy napping on his doggie bed in the living room.

Jillian cuddled their baby in her arms. When she sauntered to the couch, she lowered herself and sank down into the cushions, placing the infant in nursing position.

Anna latched on, and Riley shook his head. "How does a week-old child know how to do that?"

"God put the instinct in them." Jillian laughed. Cuddling the nursing child in her arms, she took on a serious air. "Riley, at the end of the month, I'm going back to the clinic. My two volunteers can only man it for a few more weeks. They're using vacation time. But I can take Anna with me."

"You can stay home full time with her if you want. As you know, Glover offered me a rather healthy package."

She grinned. "I know, honey. Thanks to your high GPA. But you also know how long and hard I've worked to get The Jeremiah House open. I can't abandon it now. Besides I have a good tax accountant to advise me."

Riley kissed the back of his daughter's head. "That's one thing I love about you. Your strong sense of service to the Lord. It took me too long to figure out where He was sending me."

"But you know now."

Riley kissed his wife's cheek. "I would appreciate your prayers today. I'm a little nervous."

"You are the most ambitious and responsible man I know." Jillian held out her hand to him and squeezed. "You're going to do fine. For sure, I'll be praying for you. I love you, Riley."

Kissing his baby once more, he turned toward the front door. The thirty-minute drive through traffic wasn't exactly fun. But the commute to work would be shorter when they moved into their new home next month.

One more time Riley took in the incredible view in front of him, his wife and child. "Thank you, Lord. You restored to us the years the locust ate." His heart soared with gladness.

About the author:

An award-winning author, June Foster is a retired teacher with a BA in education and MA in counseling. Her characters find themselves in tough situations but overcome through God's power and the Word. She writes edgy topics wrapped in a good story. To date, she's seen seventeen contemporary romances and several short stories published. Find June online at junefoster.com.

All Things New is book 3 in the Woodlyn series. If you missed the first two, check out Jess and Holly's story in Flawless and Tim and Roxanne's story in Out of Control.

Flawless

Though Jess Colton gave his life to the Lord, he held onto an old habit. Fueled by alcohol, he spent a night with a girl from his past, defying his Christian principles. When he quit drinking to honor God, he discovered another addiction. Now he can't manage his own life as his weight soars and diabetes threatens to claim him. Jess is baffled when the beautiful Holly Harrison declares her love.

Holly Harrison lived to please herself. But everything caught up with her in one moment of time when a destructive motorcycle accident altered her life forever. Nowhere else to turn, she looked to God for answers. Now, she's convinced no Christian man would be attracted to her. She doesn't plan on falling in love with the handsome Jess Colton seeing past his bulk to the godly, tender man within. When Jess drives a wedge between them, she loses hope of a future together.

Can Holly overcome her handicap? Can Jess find control over his eating and his life? Only God has the answer.

Out of Control

Tim Garrett saw Jess Colton back to health in *Flawless* but can't control his own life. When Woodlyn Fellowship hires Tim as the new youth pastor, he's still powerless over the uncontrollable anger he learned from his father. If he can't escape the outbursts that hold him captive, he'll lose his job. To further complicate his life, an unlikely church member devises a sinister scheme for his dismissal. Tim has one last chance at Camp Solid Rock. When he discovers a startling secret from a youthful adversary, can he save the boy's life?

Roxanne Ratner's father abandoned her as a young girl, and now she doesn't trust men. They'll only hurt her. Shopping for designer clothes is a poor substitute for the love she craves. The new Christian fights old habits of holding on to a guy. After she tempts Tim to sin, she must seek his forgiveness.
Can God cool Tim's angry heart and teach Roxanne true beauty lies within?

www.ingramcontent.com/pod-product-compliance
Lightning Source LLC
LaVergne TN
LVHW012016060526
838201LV00061B/4328